Pr ...

"Part com... ... ...
this fast-reading, playful novel takes the idea of
feeling out of place to a hilarious extreme."
—*Publishers Weekly* on *Prada and Prejudice*

"A fun and charming read, sure to be popular
with fans of humor and romance."
—*School Library Journal* on *Prada and Prejudice*

Praise for Marisa Carroll

"A heart-wrenching journey
as Justin and Sophia try to find a way to be together."
—*RT Book Reviews* on *Forbidden Attraction*

"A powerful, riveting family drama
with deftly drawn characters."
—*RT Book Reviews* on *Before Thanksgiving Comes*

MANDY HUBBARD

is the author of *Prada and Prejudice,* a novel for teens. She was born and raised in Enumclaw, Washington, where she went to high school with NASCAR driver Kasey Kahne. She lives with her husband and daughter. Visit her at www.mandyhubbard.com.

MARISA CARROLL

is the pen name of sisters Carol Wagner and Marian Franz. The team has been writing bestselling books for almost twenty-five years. During that time they have published over forty titles, many for the Harlequin Superromance line and feature and custom publishing. They are the recipients of several industry awards, including a Lifetime Achievement Award from *RT Book Reviews* and a RITA® Award nomination from Romance Writers of America, and their books have been featured on the *USA TODAY,* Waldenbooks and B. Dalton bestseller lists. The sisters live near each other in northwestern Ohio, surrounded by children, grandchildren, brothers, sisters, aunts, uncles, cousins and old and dear friends.

NASCAR®

At Any Cost

Mandy Hubbard 〜 Marisa Carroll

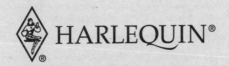

HARLEQUIN®

TORONTO • NEW YORK • LONDON
AMSTERDAM • PARIS • SYDNEY • HAMBURG
STOCKHOLM • ATHENS • TOKYO • MILAN • MADRID
PRAGUE • WARSAW • BUDAPEST • AUCKLAND

If you purchased this book without a cover you should be aware that this book is stolen property. It was reported as "unsold and destroyed" to the publisher, and neither the author nor the publisher has received any payment for this "stripped book."

ISBN-13: 978-0-373-18536-8

AT ANY COST

Copyright © 2010 by Harlequin Books S.A.

The publisher acknowledges the copyright holders of the individual works as follows:

DRIVEN
Copyright © 2010 by Harlequin Books S.A.
Mandy Hubbard is acknowledged as the author of "Driven."

LADY'S CHOICE
Copyright © 2010 by Harlequin Books S.A.
Marisa Carroll is acknowledged as the author of "Lady's Choice."

NASCAR® and the NASCAR Library Collection® are registered trademarks of the National Association for Stock Car Auto Racing, Inc.

Recycling programs for this product may not exist in your area.

All rights reserved. Except for use in any review, the reproduction or utilization of this work in whole or in part in any form by any electronic, mechanical or other means, now known or hereafter invented, including xerography, photocopying and recording, or in any information storage or retrieval system, is forbidden without the written permission of the publisher, Harlequin Enterprises Limited, 225 Duncan Mill Road, Don Mills, Ontario, Canada M3B 3K9.

This is a work of fiction. Names, characters, places and incidents are either the product of the author's imagination or are used fictitiously, and any resemblance to actual persons, living or dead, business establishments, events or locales is entirely coincidental.

This edition published by arrangement with Harlequin Books S.A.

® and TM are trademarks of the publisher. Trademarks indicated with ® are registered in the United States Patent and Trademark Office, the Canadian Trade Marks Office and in other countries.

www.eHarlequin.com

Printed in U.S.A.

CONTENTS

An excerpt from Hilton Branch's prison journal...

Every night I dream of Rose, what it was to sit with her in her mountains, to feel as though I could breathe for the first time in years. I'd give anything to see her, to talk to her one more time.

But the only way I can keep her and her daughters safe is by letting her believe that I've forsaken them. If I love her, I have to let her go.

I do love her. That much, at least, is true. Nearly everything else between us was a lie, beginning with the name Hal Walker that I used when we met, on that hunting trip to Idaho. I never expected to care about her. A waitress in a tiny town? Not my style at all, but the walls of my life had been pressing on me for some time, and she was so sweet, so uncomplicated. Women in my world always had an agenda, always wanted something from me. Even my wife Maeve wanted me, in the beginning, because she didn't want to be in charge of her daddy's bank.

Rose was a widow, young to have a teenage daughter, but she never hid from anything. Brave as could be, doing the best she knew how to care for her child in a town with no prospects. She was at peace with herself, and she made me feel peaceful, too.

But by the time I knew how important she was, I'd already lied to her too much. More than the name, there was the constant travel I said was part of my job, to excuse my long absences while I tended to the rest of my life. Then there was the marriage license we got in Mexico after I knew she was pregnant—when I was already married with four grown children of my own.

The irony is that marriage to Rose would be legal if we were doing it today, if we'd only just met. Maeve divorced me after I fled the country, and she's married to another man.

But it's too late for us now.

Biscayne Bay. I wish to God I'd never gotten involved with them. That was when the house of cards started falling. Not that it was exactly easy living two lives, each family ignorant of the existence of the other. Two years of constant lies and evasions, but I called Rose nearly every single day, no matter where I was.

Our child, my sweet Lily, only an infant the last time I saw her, would be two now. Lily loved me with a child's open heart. Amelia, Rose's older daughter, was always more lukewarm, though she liked that I made her mother happy. It's Rose, though, my Rose, the light of my life, who haunts me. If I hadn't made provisions for their future, I couldn't live with myself. Thank God I hid money for them from everyone who was after me, even the thugs at Biscayne Bay. My friend, Fred Clifton, swore he'd safeguard it even after we parted ways—for their sake, not mine. He was done with me once he caught on to the money I'd stolen from the company. He didn't understand how it was to support two families, to say nothing of one very greedy mistress.

Though as I look at that sentence now, maybe I don't, either. It all just sort of happened. I had ambitions, but what's wrong with that? A man's nothing without them. I never intended to hurt my two families. I never, ever wanted to hurt Rose. I love her so much. She's got to be wondering where I went, and I want so badly to call her.

But the only way to make amends is to stay away.

To let her forget me and move on.

They say prison is my penance. But it's not the only one.

Driven

Mandy Hubbard

For Danny, for always being there to get me out of a jam.

CHAPTER ONE

MIA CONNORS SANK INTO the cracked vinyl seat in the last available booth at Maudie's Down Home Diner. It was only noon, but her feet were throbbing from six hours at work. A month into her first full season as a full-time mechanic at Sanford Racing and the sixty-hour, six-day work weeks were already taking their toll.

Not that she had any intention of slowing down; just the opposite, in fact. It seemed every eye in North Carolina was staring at her. Being the only female mechanic in all of NASCAR made her infamous. The only way to prove herself was to work harder than any other mechanic. She couldn't just be good; she had to be great.

Right now, all she wanted was a great burger. She'd been at the shop since 6:00 a.m., and had already done an engine swap for Trey Sanford's Martinsville car and new suspension on his Texas car, among other things. Though the diner was filled with the clanging of forks and plates, Mia was convinced she could hear the ZZzzZZ sound of an air gun echoing in her ears. Sometimes, she swore she heard it as she fell asleep.

And yet despite the often bone-tired feeling as she fell into bed each night, she wouldn't give it up for the world. Everything she'd worked for was coming to fruition. Her dreams were now reality. And she was loving every frenzied minute of it.

Mia rubbed her eyes and flipped open the menu, staring down at a long list of gourmet burgers. Over the past few months, she'd gleefully tried them all. Nothing beat Maudie's burgers.

Her selection made, she slapped the menu shut and looked for her waitress. The girl was rushing by with a pot of coffee, so Mia just smiled and pushed the menu to the edge of the table as the girl scurried past. Every seat in the place was filled; Maudie's was a hot spot for the race teams in the area. It was a 1950s' style diner with classic black-and-white checkered floor, red vinyl booths and a wrap-around countertop with swiveling barstools.

Mia wondered what it looked like on weekends, when much of the team was away at the tracks. Judging by the bevy of team jackets and shop shirts, it was probably half-empty.

The door chimed, and Mia glanced up to see a tall, auburn-haired man enter, nearly filling the frame of the door. He must have been six-five, maybe six-six. He was wearing the unmistakable blue-and-white jacket of Kent Grosso's racing team, the Smoothtone Music label splashed across the chest. Even through the thick jacket, Mia could tell the man was muscular.

And familiar. She knew she'd seen him a time or two. He went over the wall, didn't he? Seems she'd seen him wearing a helmet. Was he a tire carrier? Maybe a gas man.

Mia narrowed her eyes and tried to put her finger on what she'd seen him doing. There were so many teams, so many people. She was just too focused on her team's car to notice them half the time.

"I'll be right with you," the waitress said to Mia, interrupting her thoughts.

Mia blinked. Had she been staring at him? Oh God, she had. He was walking this way now. She shrank down into the booth, obscuring the Sanford Racing logo on the front of her blue-and-yellow shop shirt.

Before she could sink far enough to disappear, he stopped in front of her booth. Up close, he had reddish-brown stubble lining his jaw and gorgeous, expressive brown eyes.

"Mind if I sit? Seems this is the last empty seat."

"Oh, uh—" Mia glanced around. He was right, of course. "Sure. Go for it."

"Thanks, Mia." He grinned at her, flashing a row of bright white teeth. Yes, she'd seen that smile before, on pit road. If only she had a name to go with it.

Mia sat up in the booth again. "How'd you know my name?"

He raised a brow. "I'd be surprised if there was a guy on pit road who didn't know it," he said.

Mia felt her face heat up. Something about the way he said it—the way he looked at her—made the room seem far too warm.

"I'm Seth, by the way. Jackman for the No. 414 car."

Mia reached a hand out to grasp his. She wasn't embarrassed by the fact it was callused, or by the grease under her nails. If he didn't like it—and most guys didn't—that was his problem. "Nice to meet you."

He nodded, shaking her hand with a firm grasp.

"Do you need my menu?" she asked, eager to turn their attention to something neutral.

He waved it away. "Nah, I always get the same thing. Hawaiian Burger with fries."

Mia nodded. "Good choice."

The waitress returned then, and Seth and Mia ordered. Mellie, her nametag read. She looked to be close to Mia's age, maybe twenty years old. She was pretty: slender, with her black hair cut in a near-pixie cut. The woman scribbled their orders on a tattered notepad, then took their menu. After Mellie walked away, Seth turned his attention to Mia. His warm brown eyes stared straight at her, and she had to force herself to stare straight back.

"What?" she said, when she couldn't take his stare any longer. What was with this guy? He waltzed in, sat down and then seemed to enjoy making her squirm.

Seth's lips curled into a slow, easy smile. "Nothing. Just wondering how a girl like you," he said, pausing and letting his eyes dip for just one moment, "ends up as a mechanic."

Mia's cheeks warmed again as she sat back against the booth. Flustered, she fingered the spot where a small pearl pendant used to lie, then realized too late it wasn't there. Jewelry was dangerous in the shop, so she never wore it anymore. In fact, she hadn't worn it in over a year, since she'd started working for Sanford. By letting all those frivolous things slide, she fit in at the shop. It worked. And it was a small price to pay. In fact, she hadn't even thought about it in weeks.

So why did Seth, just five minutes after meeting him, make her think about it?

Mia let her hands drop to her lap and nervously clasped them. She chewed her lip and tried to come up with a suitable answer to his question. People asked her about her chosen career all the time. Every day, in fact.

"Because I can," she said, staring straight into Seth's eyes, challenging him to disagree.

Seth nodded, slowly, studying Mia as if he could read between the lines if he looked long enough. He took a sip of the glass of water the waitress had set down in front of them. Every move he made was comfortable, self-assured. He wasn't the slightest bit affected by lunch with a perfect stranger. "You're not bothered being one of the only women in NASCAR who works under the hood?"

Mia raised an eyebrow and gave him a cocky smile. This was one question she enjoyed answering. Truth be told, she sort of liked the uneasy way guys seemed to take having her wrenching on the cars. It gave her an odd sense of power, as if she were in control. "No. It's not my fault the other girls would rather play with credit cards and manicures than oil pans and spark plugs. Their loss."

Mia crossed her arms, waiting for Seth to respond, waiting to see if he could handle the fact that he'd never talk her out of her chosen career. "Why? Feeling a little threatened?"

Seth pursed his lips, as if fighting a smile, but failed miserably. "I've decided I like you after all," he announced.

"After all?" Before she could stop herself, Mia snorted. "You like me *in spite* of my career?"

Seth set his glass down and leaned forward until he was halfway across the table. "I like you *because* of your career. Takes a secure woman to work in a shop full of guys. Although I'm sure there's more to you than cars, of course," he added. "There's certainly more to *me* than that."

"Oh really," Mia said, uncrossing her arms and leaning forward until their faces were just an inch apart. She was eager to turn the attention toward him. "Enlighten me."

Seth sat up and pondered his answer, staring at the ceiling with his mouth screwed to the side, tapping on his chin as if it took great thought. "Well, I enjoy baking. I make legendary coconut macaroons."

"Really?" Mia said, the surprise evident in her voice.

"No," he said, grinning. "I'm a terrible cook. I burn frozen pizza."

"Oh," Mia said with a laugh.

"But I am *excellent* at ordering takeout."

"A valuable skill." Mia picked up a fork and used it to start picking at her napkin. If she looked at him any longer, she was going to lean straight over and kiss him. He was just *that* alluring. Every time he smiled at her, it got a little harder to breathe.

"It is. Did you know that on Tuesdays, tacos are two for one at Miguel's?"

Mia smirked, still staring at the fork. "I had no clue."

"And the paper prints a twenty-percent-off coupon for Happy Teriyaki every Wednesday."

"Astounding."

Seth sighed. "Okay, I can see you're not impressed."

Mia looked up from the table. Seth's expression was one of exaggerated defeat. Was he always this playful? "Whatever gave you that idea?"

"Probably your smirk."

Mia tried to force a neutral expression, but she couldn't keep her lips from twitching.

Seth tapped his fingers on the table and looked around, as if taking in the various team jackets. An easy silence settled over the table.

"So what's it like working at the Sanford shop?" Seth asked.

"Oh, uh-uh. I'm not giving away any secrets. *Especially* not to a Grosso team member."

"I'm not a spy, I swear," he said, his expression one of embellished innocence. With his eyes wide like they were, Mia could see golden flecks that caught the light.

"That's exactly what a spy would say." Mia leaned in, narrowing her eyes, feigning complete seriousness. "Who sent you?"

"You have a point." Seth crossed his arms, considering this. "Okay, I admit it." He leaned in across the table and motioned for Mia to come closer. She leaned toward him, until his lips were near her temple, almost brushing her ear. Then he whispered, "It was the muffin man."

Mia rolled her eyes and sat up, but she couldn't keep her lips from twitching.

So Seth was funny.

And really, really attractive. His smile was just the tiniest bit crooked when he was trying not to laugh, which gave him a sort of rugged quality. But when he grinned widely, it became flawless, all sparkling white teeth.

A few minutes later, Mellie arrived with their burgers. Had they been talking that long already? A glance at the clock revealed it had been ten minutes since he'd sat down. Talking to Seth proved to be just like working on an engine: totally engrossing.

Mia reached for the ketchup bottle just as Seth grabbed it, brushing his fingertips. Seth popped the top off and handed it to her.

"Ladies first."

Mia nodded and took the bottle, trying not to look overly pleased. Sure, she wanted to be treated just like any other guy in NASCAR. But yet she couldn't deny that she liked the way Seth looked at her—as if somehow, even through the standard-issue Sanford Racing shirt and loose-fitting shop pants, he found her sexy.

Mia hadn't felt like that in almost two years, since she'd started wearing those boring black shoes and loose-fitting shop slacks. Sure, she was a tomboy even in high school, but she still managed to wear jeans that fit well, still tried to keep the dirt out from under her nails.

But she refused to be a distraction at the shop, so she did everything she could to blend in. And that meant going unnoticed.

Yet Seth was looking at her as if he *did* notice her, and it was warming her from the inside out, making her feel as if the shop uniform were invisible.

Ten minutes later, when Seth licked his lips, Mia had to stop herself from doing the same thing. They'd been laughing and joking nonstop as they were eating, and she'd caught herself leaning in toward him time and again. He was charismatic, she'd give him that. And when he started talking about his team, his eyes took on a light that made her wish the conversation would never end. He was driven. Anyone could see it.

When Mellie came by with the tab, Seth handed the waitress a twenty before Mia could blink.

"You didn't have to—"

"I want to," he said, smiling and waving her away, as if it was nothing.

"Thank you." Mia grabbed her jacket from the seat and stood up to put it on. Seth reached over and unfolded the crumpled collar, and Mia froze as his skin touched hers. His fingers brushed against her for a moment, but it was enough to make the hairs on the back of her neck stand on end.

She smiled at him, hoping he didn't see her shiver as a chill raced down her spine, and walked toward the door, Seth trailing after her.

Halfway to the door, she heard someone say goodbye to him as he walked by. If the woman's looks were anything like her voice, she was sultry, sexy…

Mia shook her head. They were at a café popular with racing teams. And Seth was a single, attractive guy. It wasn't as if he were invisible. Of course he had friends. Even those of the female variety.

Outside, it was still a little cool. Spring would be here soon. Mia looked forward to it, and the rest of the NASCAR Sprint Cup Series season. She was one of the B-team mechanics for Trey Sanford, traveling with the team, working on his car in the garage. She didn't touch it on the track, but maybe, if she worked hard enough, long enough, she'd be an A-team member within a few seasons. For now, she was absorbing everything she could, learning more at every race. She'd see most of the country before the final event in Homestead this coming fall. Texas, California, New York… She couldn't wait to drink it all in.

Last year, she'd arrived in NASCAR, and there was only one way to go from here: up. To the top, to the A team, to being the best.

"So, where are we going on our second date?" Seth asked, as they headed into the parking lot.

Mia froze, one foot in the gravel lot, one still on the concrete walkway. "Oh, I mean, you seem nice, but—"

"Already seeing someone?" Seth stopped in front of her, fishing his car keys out of his pocket.

"Well, no, it's just, I'm trying to focus on my career right now. I have a lot to prove." Mia wanted to cringe just saying the words out loud, no matter how true it was. "I mean, you knew who I was, just because I'm the girl mechanic. People are watching me, you know?"

Mia's mother, even through her failing health, had scraped together the family's last dime to put her through a racing technical program, and her sister, Cassie, had sacrificed just as much to get her the job at Sanford Racing. And it wasn't just them, either. Mia had done everything in her power to succeed. She'd studied harder, worked longer, transformed herself into someone who would fit in at the shop and at the track. She wanted this career with a passion she couldn't put into words. After all it had taken to get her here, she wasn't going to lose her focus. Not now.

Besides, a charming guy like Seth? He'd definitely distract her. He'd made the past half hour fly by as if in fast forward.

Seth said nothing, just stared at her. Mia had no choice but to fill the silence.

"I haven't been at Sanford very long, and it's my first season as a full-time mechanic, and I don't want to—"

Seth placed a hand, lightly, on her shoulder, and she stopped babbling. She could no longer feel her toes, just the spot where his hand rested on her shoulder, burning through the team jacket.

"Relax. We'll catch up in Bristol, I'm sure." His hand slipped off her shoulder, and he shrugged. "See you, Mia."

Mia nodded and watched him walk away, his boots crunching in the gravel as he approached his white pickup truck. She seemed to be frozen, and it wasn't until he glanced back at her that she realized she was just standing there, staring.

He gave her an arrogant, lazy grin, as if he knew she was berating herself for turning him down, and then climbed in his truck, fired it up and drove away. Mia still couldn't seem to move, even after it had disappeared around a corner.

"You coulda said yes, you know," someone said.

Mia jumped and turned to see Sheila, the redheaded woman who owned Maudie's. She was clad in a black apron, tossing a couple trash bags in the Dumpster next to the building.

"You heard that?" Mia asked, cringing. She didn't know Sheila beyond the diner, and yet the woman's wise, motherly vibe always made Mia want to spill all of her troubles. No matter how busy the diner, Sheila always had time to chat.

Sheila nodded. "Yeah. Seems a guy that attractive asks me out, I say yes."

Mia rubbed a hand across her face and groaned. "I know. It's just I have a lot on my plate. New job. I need to focus."

And it was true. Maybe next year…

"You sound like Mellie."

"The waitress?"

Sheila nodded and pointed toward the bustling restaurant. "Strong resemblance, don't you think?"

Mia looked through the windows at Mellie. Her shoulders were hunched as she bused a table, her hands moving at warp speed, her apron already covered in yellow mustard stains even though it was barely 12:30 p.m. She *was* rather pretty, but the stress was showing. Even from the parking lot, Mia could nearly see the weight pressing down on the girl.

She hated to admit that Mellie looked a lot like Mia felt.

"I own the place, and I don't worry that much. Mellie needs to get out more. I think Bart Branch is interested in her—he's always here. I know he loves my food but that's not it. I keep telling her that, but she says she needs to *focus on her responsibilities*. Sound a little familiar?"

Mia's eyes narrowed as she looked back at Sheila. "I don't look *that* bad, do I?"

Sheila shrugged.

Dang. Mia blew out a long, slow sigh. She had to admit, Sheila had a point. She'd entered the tech program straight out of high school and had been so focused on acing the courses, she'd turned down any invitations for a date. Her focus had only intensified during her employment at Sanford.

Lunch with Seth had been the closest thing to a date she'd had in months.

"It's okay to have a little fun once in a while," Sheila said. Mia locked eyes with her for a long moment, until she found herself grinning back at the older woman.

"Okay, okay. If he asks me again, I'll say yes."

"Thatta girl."

Mia sighed in resignation, but the smile didn't leave her face. "For now, though, I gotta get back to work."

"Okay. Come back soon, hon."

"Sure." Mia walked away, feeling a little funny about discussing something like this with a woman who was hardly more than a stranger, but also, maybe, a little glad. Maybe all she needed was a little push.

Maybe it was a little like needing *permission* to have a little fun, but Mia didn't really care. Sheila had made a good point, and Mia was already wondering when she'd see Seth again.

The Bristol race was only three days away. If Seth talked to her—if he wanted to share a lunch break—she'd have to say yes.

She had to eat, didn't she?

Her job could survive a simple lunch.

Assuming he asked, of course.

CHAPTER TWO

SETH LEANED AGAINST the concrete barrier on pit road, shielding his eyes from the rising sun as the No. 414 car flew by out on the track. Two laps earlier, his crew had adjusted the sway bar, and it looked as if their efforts had paid off. Kent Grosso, driver of the No. 414 car, had just picked up three-tenths on the last lap.

Seth grinned as he wiped the sweat from his brow. There was nothing like the track, even if it was only practice.

Once, NASCAR hadn't been anything more than a sport on television. He'd been a hockey player, plain and simple. He belonged on the ice. And he was good.

But not good enough to go pro, and he had to pay the bills. His buddy Nate had been the one to tell him about pit crews, and how the members were athletes, plain and simple. He'd been skeptical, but he'd gone and checked it out. Nate had made it sound unforgettable, exciting, just the kind of thing he'd fall in love with.

And Nate had been right—Seth had been hooked the moment he set foot on the track. The team became his passion. Whether it was the fourteen—or if they were really on top of their game, thirteen—seconds of utter concentration during pit stops, or sitting on the wall, nerves on edge, watching his car, he couldn't get enough. The team was his life.

And Nate was right about another thing: every member of the crew was an athlete. Seth often felt just as worn-out after a race as he had after a game on the ice. Every second during a pit stop mattered. Their car could only gain in tenths of a second while on the track, but during a pit stop it could gain—or lose—whole seconds.

Seth felt a little on edge today. Bristol was an intense, tiny track, just half a mile long. The haulers parked mere inches from one another. The stands at this track towered over the racing surface and wrapped around it completely, like a football field or a baseball stadium. Standing in the middle of the place, down by the pits, Seth could spin around 360 degrees and see nothing but the stands and the crowd.

Today, there was only a smattering of fans. Most of them would come in on Sunday, steadily filling the seats until it was a sea of faces and colors.

Bristol always sold out. It was one of the best weekends in the NASCAR Sprint Cup Series. The racing was competitive, exciting and action-packed. By the time the drivers reached the last few dozen laps, the entire place would be on its feet, and the roar of the fans would nearly overpower the hum of the engines.

So far it seemed they were on track for a good qualifying run later that afternoon. They'd drawn one of the last runs, which was perfect. As the track cooled, their car would tighten up, exactly what it needed. With a little luck, they might even take the pole.

The car came in early from practice, as Kent was happy with the way it drove. The majority of the field was still hot on the racing surface as his car returned to the garage, and Seth turned toward something else entirely: food. It had been hours since breakfast, and he was ready for something to fill the grumbling void in his stomach.

Of course, there was another reason he was thinking about lunch.

Ever since Mia had declined another chance to get together, he'd wanted nothing else but to see her again.

He'd seen her around the track before. She was hard to miss, in fact. He'd been intrigued by the idea of her working on the car. Impressed, even. So when he'd seen his chance to share a lunch break with her, he'd jumped on it.

And lunch with her had been...mesmerizing. Just thinking of her, of the way her eyes lit up when she talked about her team, of the way she threw her head back when she laughed...

Seth wanted to see more of her. Maybe today would be the day.

He ambled toward the garage, hoping to spot the blue-and-yellow colors of Trey Sanford's car. Halfway back to his team's garage, Seth's eyes encountered the familiar face he'd been hoping to see: Mia. He couldn't help the way his lips lifted a little at the sight of her. She was wearing her shop shirt and slacks, her hair back in a loose bun with pieces escaping and brushing the back of her neck. She was sitting on a rolling stool in the center of the garage, talking to another mechanic on the Sanford team. Their car was obviously still on the track, which meant Mia was awaiting its return so that they could make some changes.

Seth glanced at his watch. There was thirty minutes left in practice. Assuming the car didn't retire early like his did—or duck into the shop for some big changes—she could have lunch with him.

And lunch with Mia was infinitely better than lunch with the guys.

Seth headed toward the Sanford garage, unable to contain his smile as he heard her laugh at something the other mechanic said, her shoulders shaking as she hunched over. She was undeniably attractive when she let her guard down. Seth wasn't sure why the wall went up when he asked her out in the parking lot of Maudie's, but he hoped it wouldn't reappear now.

He was barely into the shop door when the other mechanic saw him and stood up. Was he defensive about having a Grosso crew member standing in his garage, or was it meant simply to be polite?

Seth gave him an easy wave, letting him know he was more friend than foe. "Hey. Mind if I steal Mia for a little lunch?"

Mia sat up straighter, clearly surprised. Seth had trouble reading anything beyond that. Was she pleased or annoyed?

Then she shook her head, and Seth got his answer. "You know I can't. The car will be back soon."

"In thirty minutes," he said.

"And what if something breaks? Or if they come in early and I'm not here?"

There was a slight edge to her voice that Seth couldn't help but recognize. She wouldn't risk going to lunch when she was on duty. Not by a long shot. She wasn't kidding when she said she took her job seriously.

Then again, if she asked him to lunch when the track was hot, and he was needed in the pit stall, he'd probably react the same way.

"Later, then? Before qualifying?"

"Go ahead, Mia. The car's not coming in any time soon, and you skipped breakfast. I'm tired of listening to your stomach grumble. You've got twenty minutes, at least."

Mia turned back to look at the mechanic behind her—

a dark-haired man in his mid-thirties—and her bangs slid into her face.

When she turned to face him again, she just smiled a little and slid off the stool. Seth was surprised at the shot of pleasure that coursed through him as he realized she was going to have lunch with him. Whatever it was that made her special, he was officially entranced.

He waited at the door for her, and then the two of them walked down the garage area a bit until they found a vendor selling sandwiches. Seth selected ham, and Mia turkey, then they gathered up sodas and chips and found a nearby table, a red-and-white umbrella casting shade over the seats. It was uncharacteristically warm for Bristol's spring race, and the shade was welcome, especially given Seth's uniform.

Silence settled over the table, though it wasn't entirely uncomfortable. They chewed on their sandwiches and sipped on their drinks. Seth tried to think of something charming to say to get Mia to loosen up, but ultimately came up empty. He settled for their middle ground: work.

"How's the car?" Seth asked.

Mia shrugged. It was different, seeing such small shoulders filling out the shop shirt like she did. Women worked in NASCAR all the time—but it was usually in the offices. Seth wondered if she had trouble finding a shop shirt that small.

The lack of women in the sport wasn't because NASCAR didn't want them in the garages or the cars. Quite the opposite, in fact. There were driver development programs for them, and the tech schools welcomed everyone with open arms, trying to diversify the personnel working within the NASCAR Sprint Cup Series. But that didn't mean women came running to sign up to be a mechanic. Mia was the first one he'd ever met.

No wonder he was intrigued.

"It's not bad. A little loose. They're working on it, but we'll have our job cut out for us. Just glad its not an impound race."

Seth nodded. He wasn't wild about impound races, either, even if he wasn't a mechanic. At the impound races, the car couldn't be touched after qualifying—the one that rolled across the line as the green flag dropped was the same one they'd run to qualify. The idea was that the teams wouldn't have to work so hard—or so many hours—to make changes.

It saved the teams money, sure, but they also made it a challenge to have a good car at the start of the race. And a messed-up car meant a lot of pit stops. Stops he would lead, being the jackman. The responsibility would fall on him to keep the team moving through a fast stop.

Then again, he did love a challenge. And when the team kept things going, stop after stop, it was an adrenaline rush like he'd never known.

"We've been picking up a bit on the track. We should have a good qualifying run."

Mia nodded. "Your times are faster than ours so far." She got a far-off look for a moment, and he could see she was thinking about their car. He could practically see her wheels turning as she thought it over, dissecting the car, thinking about the changes she could make when it came back to the garage.

It was as if Mia didn't exist outside work, as if a mechanic was all she'd let herself be.

If she kept it up, this would be one quiet lunch.

"So, where you from?" he asked, steering her back toward him.

"Charlotte, born and raised. You?"

"New England. Moved to Charlotte a few years ago thanks to the persuasion of a friend."

"Do you like it?"

He thought about the long, cold, beautiful winters of New England. "Yeah. But I wish I had the chance for more outdoor ice skating like I used to."

"Ice skating?" Mia sat up and gave him a skeptical look, her head tilted to the side. There was something else in her eyes, too: amusement.

When she actually met his eyes, she proved easy to read. It was too bad she was always evading his looks.

"I played hockey through college."

"Oh," she said. "I was picturing figure skating. I knew that didn't sound right."

Seth tried to act indignant, puffing up his chest and crossing his arms. "Are you saying I'm not graceful enough to pull it off? I assure you, I am master of the triple axel."

Mia laughed. "It's not that I don't think you are… graceful," she said, pausing to let her eyes sweep over him. "Just more that you look too large for a skater. Hockey makes sense."

"Whew. Because I don't want to give off the wrong impression. I'm trying out for *The Lion King on Ice* next week."

Mia laughed again and then covered her mouth, clearly embarrassed, as it was currently full of potato chips. She paused just long enough to swallow. "You're a shoo-in for one of the giraffes."

"Thank you. That was the part I was especially hopeful for. The giraffe is a very esteemed position."

Mia stifled a giggle and just nodded. "Any family living in Charlotte with you?"

"No wife, if that's what you're asking," he said, staring straight into her eyes. *Was* that what she was asking?

No, by her reaction, it wasn't, but he didn't regret saying it, just the same.

Mia blushed and looked down at her sandwich. "No, I was talking about brothers, sisters. That kind of thing. NASCAR is often a family affair."

Of course that's what she meant.

"I'm an only child. My folks still live up north. Visit them during the holidays. You know as well as anyone else how busy we are. Sometimes they make it down, but my mom hates flying. You?"

"My mom lives in Charlotte. And my sister married Ethan Hunt, so I see her more than necessary," Mia said, smiling at the last comment.

"Cassie is your sister?"

Mia nodded.

"I didn't realize that. That's great. They seem very happy. She hangs out on the pit box, you'd think Ethan would at least have her calculating fuel mileage by now," he said.

Mia grinned. "He's probably working on that." She paused for a moment, obviously considering her sister and Ethan. "I almost never see one without the other. It's amazing…or maybe annoying, watching them. They're so ridiculously in love nothing else exists."

Seth turned to his potato chips, as he had little to say on the subject of love. Had he ever experienced it? Maybe, years ago, but as he was traveling with the hockey team, it eventually drifted away from him. Ever since, he'd just had his fun, enjoyed life. Dated, as it were.

And for now, he was happy with the status quo: light, breezy dates. No strings attached, no one to worry about at home. The NASCAR Sprint Cup Series kept him on the road at least thirty-six weeks a year, even longer than his pseudoathletic career had. There was simply no way to maintain a relationship. If he had a girl waiting for him at home, he would just feel guilty.

It worked better this way.

"Speaking of giraffes…jelly beans or chocolate eggs?"

Mia snorted. "That sentence makes no sense."

Seth just smiled at her. "I know, it's part of my charm, don't you think?"

"That you make no sense?"

"Yes."

She just smiled and met his gaze for a long moment. "I suppose so."

"So you *do* find me charming."

She dropped her jaw, but her lips twitched, and it ended up turning into a smile. "Maybe. If I say yes, will it increase your ever-growing ego?"

"Of course."

"Then I find you to be the least charming man I've ever met."

"You're just jealous that I look so great in my uniform," Seth said, gesturing to his blue-and-white fire-retardant suit. He'd unzipped it to the waist, revealing the white turtleneck underneath.

"I wear shop clothes," she pointed out.

"That's why you're jealous," he said.

She shook her head, still smiling. "However did you guess?"

Seth's phone rang then, and he set his sandwich down to dig it out. It took him only a second to silence it and shove it back in his pocket.

"One of your many admirers?" Mia asked.

"Nah, just my mom," Seth said, squirming a little.

It *had* been a girl. One he'd gone out with two weeks ago. Their date had been the most boring two hours of his life. She'd prattled on and on about some kind of specialty hair cream she'd found in Milan.

"Nice try, but I don't buy that." Mia picked up a potato chip, considered it for a moment and then tossed it at him.

It nailed him between the eyes. Seth blinked once, twice and then stared at her. Unlike the girl who'd just called him, Mia could never be considered *boring*. "I can't believe you just did that."

Mia shrugged. "Just had to knock you down a peg."

Her smile was so wide and playful that Seth couldn't keep from laughing. He took a long sip of his soda to regain his composure.

"I'd like to take you out," he said, out of the blue.

He could see he'd caught her off guard. The smile melted and she just stared at him. She had that look that said he was about to be rejected.

"I don't know. I mean, I'd like to, and you're a really great guy, it's just—"

"You have to focus on your job?" he said.

By the way she snapped her jaw shut, he knew he'd nailed it. "You don't work twenty-four hours a day."

She blinked several times, seemed to be considering her options. "I know, and I've had fun during lunch. But lunch is one thing, and a relationship is another. I already feel like a bit of an outsider in the shop. And if I add dating a Grosso team member to the list of reasons I'm different…"

"So don't tell them. It's none of their business who you date."

"Charlotte may be a big city, but they'd find out."

"Not for what I have in mind."

She paused, and he knew he had her.

"And what do you have in mind?" she asked.

"It's a surprise. You'll find out on Tuesday."

She tipped her head to the side, a smile winning out. "So sure I'll accept?"

Seth scribbled down an address and handed it to Mia. "Meet me here when you get off. Don't bother changing out of your shop uniform."

Mia narrowed her eyes. "Now I'm intrigued."

Seth grinned and looked straight at her. "I knew you would be." He glanced at his watch. Their twenty minutes was up. "But it looks like lunch is over," he said, showing her his watch.

"Really?" She leaned across the table to get a better look. "Wow. Okay, I'd better go."

She tossed her empty soda can into the recycling bin and stood, a little awkwardly, in front of him. "Thanks for lunch."

"Yep."

She started to scurry away, but Seth called out to her. "And Mia?"

She turned, looking at him with raised brows.

"See you Tuesday."

She just rolled her eyes. "I haven't accepted yet."

"You will."

She shook her head and turned back toward the garage, disappearing around the corner.

Seth hoped he was right. Because he knew if she did, she wouldn't regret it.

And neither would he.

CHAPTER THREE

MIA SLID OUT FROM underneath the car and sat up on the creeper, tucking a few errant strands of hair behind her ear. The clock over the door to Ethan's office read 4:50 p.m., edging ever closer to quitting time.

She still hadn't decided whether she was going to show up at the mystery address, and now it was time to pack up her tools. Her stomach fluttered as she coiled up the hose on her air gun. The men around her were tossing wrenches into toolboxes and slipping sockets back into their designated spots.

"Did you need help with that?"

Mia turned to face Brian, a ten-year-vet at Sanford Racing. He was a member of the A team, a position Mia aspired to. In his late thirties, he had thinning dark hair, and his lips were pursed in a thin line as his dark, intense eyes narrowed. He had a sort of hard look, one that Mia didn't care for. The other guys, they were warm; goofy, even. They accepted her.

Brian was different.

"With the air hose?" She raised a brow and looked at the coiled hose.

Something about Brian always put her on guard. He had a strange, quasi-passive-aggressive nature about him that no one else seemed to pick up on. Most of the time, Mia figured she was being paranoid.

He shook his head. "With the suspension."

"Oh. Uh, no, actually, I'm done."

"Are you sure?" He crossed his arms. He was standing in front of her, blocking the path to where she'd hung up the tools.

Mia froze, her hand still on the coiled air hose. The team members around them continued to pick up, oblivious to the tug-of-war that Mia always seemed to be playing with Brian. "Yes. I'm sure. You can check it if you want."

He simply stared at her for a second longer than normal, and then walked away.

She didn't get him. And after such a long day, she wasn't in the mood to analyze his abrasive behavior.

She'd rather analyze Seth's more charming behavior.

Who was she kidding, pretending she wasn't sure whether she'd meet up with him tonight? She'd been thinking about him all day. And she wanted to find out what he had in mind for their mystery date.

He must have known that she couldn't resist finding out. The guy was simply too smooth for his own good. And while that was a little disconcerting, she couldn't deny that this time, he won. She was going to go.

She washed up, grimacing at her reflection in the mirror. He'd said she should show up in her uniform. Did he realize that meant sweaty, matted hair and zero makeup?

It was too late for a backup plan. This morning she'd been so convinced she'd chicken out that she hadn't grabbed what makeup she owned, and there wasn't enough time to dash home.

She headed out to her trusty ten-year-old coupe, punching

the address into the GPS navigator on her phone. Whatever the address was, it was six miles from the shop, in what Mia was fairly certain was an industrial area. Interesting.

Her nerves intensified as she drove across town. Was she crazy to do this? To meet a stranger at a mystery address?

But it was too late to change her mind. The navigator told her that her destination was on the left, and she pulled into the parking lot. What was this place? It looked like any other warehouse. There was no sign along the road or mounted on the building, only some tall white numbers spelling out an address.

Seth's white truck was in the lot, and as she pulled into a parking stall, he stepped out. She tried to concentrate on parking the car, as if it took every ounce of effort to set the brake and turn off the headlights.

He was standing at her car while she still fumbled with her keys, and he swung open her door before she knew what she'd say to him.

"You came," he said.

"I did."

And then she was smiling, unsure of why she'd been so worried. Seth was wearing jeans with a plain white T-shirt and a team jacket. A ball cap was slung low over his eyes, making them seem darker. But when he smiled at her, it was as if they glowed.

He was happy to see her. The thought made her insides feel warm. He didn't even have to compliment her and yet she felt more attractive. It was strange.

"So what's this all about?" she asked, trying to keep her thoughts at bay.

He reached a hand out. "Let me show you."

Pushing away her nerves, she reached out and accepted

his hand. It wasn't nearly as uncomfortable as she'd expected. He hung on to her as they stepped through the steel door and into the enormous warehouse. She liked the feeling of her hand in his, of the way he grabbed hold of it as if it wasn't a big deal at all.

Mia blinked a few times, until her eyes adjusted to the darker interior. And then she just gaped. "A go-kart track?"

Seth grinned. "A buddy owns the place. You seem like a competitive person. I thought it might be fun."

She turned to look at the challenge sparkling in his eyes and found herself smiling back at him. Maybe they'd only spent about an hour in each other's company, but he certainly had her pegged. She put a hand on her hip and leaned into him. "You're going down. You know that, right?"

He laughed. "Good to see I was right."

She followed him across the track, and they selected two go-karts. Mia stood to the side as Seth grabbed the pull-cords and fired them up. To Mia's trained ears, they ran perfectly, purring like a couple of kittens. Or maybe cougars, as it were, as these didn't seem to be garden-variety go-karts.

Mia raised an eyebrow. "Let me guess: your buddy works in NASCAR?"

Seth grinned sheepishly. "Maybe."

Mia laughed. "Do we need to wear helmets?"

"That depends. Do you plan on wrecking me?"

"I don't plan on going easy, if that's what you're asking."

Seth's eyes sparkled when he looked at her. He actually *wanted* her to race hard. She felt something swell inside her. Somehow he liked the very thing that made her more like the guys.

"Maybe helmets aren't a bad idea."

Mia laughed again, accepting the bright blue helmet

that he tossed her way. "How do I know you're not taking the better car?"

"We could trade."

"But then my helmet won't match my car and *then* whatever will I do?" she asked, a hand over her heart, as if fashion was of the utmost importance.

"Get in the green car," Seth said, shaking his head, his lips curling into an adorable crooked smile.

This was going to be fun. Maybe the most fun she'd had in months. Mia couldn't stop grinning as she climbed into the kart, buckling the harness and tightening the straps. She tapped on the gas, still holding the brake, and her grin only got bigger as the engine roared, vibrating the seat, and the tires broke loose for a second and started to burn out. Someone had spent a bit of time and money souping these things up.

And then before`she could do a thing, Seth took off, the tires screeching as he flew right by her.

"Cheater!" she hollered after him, throwing the car into gear and spinning out as she raced after him.

Seth was halfway around the first turn by the time she entered the track, but he wasn't getting off that easy. Mia nearly skidded out of control as she rounded the turn, but in seconds she was making up ground. And when he dared to pause and look back, his eyes widened to realize how fast she'd caught up.

She laughed maniacally as she came up alongside of him. Her cheeks nearly hurt from all the smiling. "You should have told me you race dirty!"

"I don't—" but before he could finish, she jerked the wheel hard left and knocked into the steel side bumper of Seth's car. The force was enough to bump Seth toward the tires mounted around the edges of the track. He bounced off and his car began to drift out of control. Seth had to crank the wheel, and just as the car started to spin the wrong way, he was able to right it.

Mia turned forward again and stomped the gas pedal to the floor, her head nearly snapping back at the quick increase of momentum.

Even so, Seth caught up, bumping her from behind, and she shrieked every time she felt the rough tap. The wheel wanted to turn toward the wall, but she just tightened her grip and kept the car on track.

Seth managed to dodge inside on a corner, coming up alongside of her. She met his eyes for only a moment before jerking the wheel hard and smashing into him. For one second, before the world blurred and the cars lost control, their eyes met.

And she knew in an instant he was loving this as much as she was.

The cars spun. Mia could only watch as the scenery swirled around her once, then twice, before the car skidded and sputtered to a stop. She looked over to see Seth's car was backward, and he was staring right at her.

And then she burst out laughing, and Seth's grin widened. She unclipped her helmet and set it in her lap.

"So where are we going on our next date?"

CHAPTER FOUR

MIA SAT ON THE CARPETED floor of her apartment, in between the open bifold doors of her closet. She'd only unpacked her boxes two months ago, when she moved in, and she still wasn't sure where she'd put half her things. Somewhere in the deep recesses of the space, there were a few dresses. And maybe a lone pair of high heels.

You wouldn't know it, though, to see the shop shirts and slacks and blue jeans and T-shirts that hung near the front. With each month, it seemed the few girlie clothes she owned were relegated ever farther back, forlorn, wrinkled and forgotten. She couldn't even remember the last time she'd worn a dress, let alone shopped for one. It must have been in high school.

Today, though, she was in the mood to find something else, something feminine, to wear. Why not? A celebration called for a little dressing up. Gina Hall, an old high-school friend, was turning twenty-one. She hadn't seen the girl in a while, but they had the sort of friendship that didn't require constant attention. Lately they got by with lots of e-mails and texting. It would be great to see each other in person.

Sometime between a hot shower and scrubbing the grease from beneath her nails, she'd decided to pamper herself. She'd already painted her nails a bright red, shaved her legs, put on makeup and curled her hair.

She'd never been a big fan of dresses, but she hadn't forgotten the power she felt when she slipped one on. She felt like someone else, like…

A woman, instead of one of the guys. And tonight, she wanted that. She wanted to step outside herself and be the girlie girl.

And she wasn't fooling herself if she tried to pretend she wasn't sure where the inspiration to do so had come from.

Seth.

Every time she was around him, she felt an odd mix of confidence and self-consciousness. The way he looked at her made her feel both sexy and awkward. Sexy, because he didn't veil the attraction he had for her. Awkward, because she felt…

Out of her league?

Seth was a guy who got noticed. At a muscular six-five, he was one of the most masculine guys she'd met in a long time. The term *ruggedly handsome* kept springing to mind.

And every time she was around him, she saw firsthand that she wasn't the only girl to take notice of him.

Why was he paying any attention to her, of all people? With Seth, it was as if he saw past the mechanic to the woman, and it completely unnerved her. Two years of nonstop grease and wrenches, and he saw none of it. She could lose herself in the conversations with him. Whenever their eyes met, she wanted to simply stare back at him, and the world seemed to disappear around them for that one simple second.

And she liked it. Because for so long, she'd been just a mechanic. Nothing else, just a mechanic. She'd stopped wearing her favorite pearldrop necklace, stopped wearing so much as lipgloss and started working every extra hour she could.

Was it so wrong to want to be something else, just for a moment? To be the girl in the room that made a few heads turn? To cut loose and have a little fun?

The time she'd spent with Seth was an experiment of sorts. A shot at being something outside of work. And it had been fun.

So why not try it again? Tonight, no one's job was at stake. She could have fun and cut loose. She herself had turned twenty-one just a few weeks ago and had hardly gone out yet. Her sister Cassie had taken her out that night for her inaugural drink, but even then, she hadn't stayed out late.

So, for the occasion, she was going to hit the bar and do just what Seth did: look at herself in a new light. As a woman. One who wasn't afraid of a short hemline and a little eyeliner.

Besides, she needed something to busy her hands and keep herself from thinking about him too much. No doubt, he was out with another girl tonight, not dwelling on memories of Mia. Not thinking that she'd had more fun at that stupid go-kart track than she'd had in a year.

Mia sat up onto her knees and crawled halfway into the closet, climbing over a dozen pairs of boring, sensible shoes to get to the back. She grabbed the lonely pair of heels and flung them over her shoulder, into her bedroom. Then she reached up toward the few skirts and dresses that she owned and yanked them off the hangers, letting them tumble down around her and then gathering them up in her arms.

Crawling backward out of the closet, she rolled back onto her butt and sat down to see what she'd come up with:

a bright sundress, too light for this time of year; a smart blue suit-dress, too serious for a night on the town; and a little black dress, one she knew hit her midthigh and showed off just a hint of cleavage.

Perfect.

Mia regarded the only pair of heels she owned: electric-blue peep-toe wedge sandals. They would make the dress appear a little more casual and add a splash of color.

Then she grinned.

Tonight, Mia the mechanic would be nowhere in sight.

SETH PUSHED THE DOOR of Andre's Bar and Grill open, then held it as two women exited the establishment. One of them looked vaguely familiar, and when she caught his eye, she nodded at him. Hmm. He must have bought her a drink at one point. It seems her name started with an R…Rachel? Rita?

His buddy Nate, gas man for the No. 414 car and the one who'd helped him get hired, followed closely on his heels as they headed toward the bar.

It had been a long, busy day, and he was ready for a drink.

Since his date with Mia two days ago, he couldn't stop thinking about her. He'd had more fun that night than on any other date—ever. Just thinking about the way she grinned at him moments before ramming into his kart made him smile.

Mia was the perfect mixture: a career-oriented girl who knew how to laugh; a sexy girl who didn't mind getting dirty; a smart girl who didn't mind acting goofy.

She was, to put it bluntly, the very opposite of the girls he usually dated. If anyone had asked Nate what Seth's type was, he'd probably say a leggy blonde. At six-five, Seth usually went for the taller girls.

And yet Mia, almost a full foot shorter than him, couldn't have been more alluring if she tried. There was so much more to her than what was on the surface, so much depth and intensity.

Andre's was more crowded than usual. A few Happy Birthday banners hung from one rafter to another, and a pink tablecloth had been spread across the two biggest tables in the place. A crowd of people mingled around an oversize, half-eaten cake.

Around here, it wasn't uncommon to have events and parties in the middle of the week instead of a Friday or Saturday like any normal person would. Although in NASCAR everyone worked Monday through Friday, the main work came on weekends with races being on Sunday—or the occasional Saturday night.

Today it looked like a group of girls in their early twenties. Nate's eyes sparkled mischievously as he nodded in their direction, his wheels already turning. Seth stifled the urge to laugh and headed for an empty space at the bar, Nate taking a seat beside him. He ordered a draft beer, and thirty seconds after the first sip, life was good again. He could feel the tension unwinding, melting into the barstool, never to be seen again.

One could hope.

"It was nice to be in Victory Lane again," Nate said, sipping from his own frosty glass.

"Especially when we played such a big role," Seth said.

"Cheers to that," Nate said, knocking his mug into Seth's.

Kent Grosso—and the No. 414 team—had won the Bristol race, thanks to good driving and pit strategy. Seth had led his teammates to the win, and their final stop had barely topped thirteen seconds.

Seth traced his finger over the condensation on his mug, a smile on his face. NASCAR was definitely the home for him. Everything about it fit.

Before he had a chance to truly relax, a woman stepped up to the bar and his pulse quickened. Her silky, slightly wavy brown hair brushed her shoulders, and her little black dressed hugged every perfect curve. She wasn't tall, and yet her legs went on for miles. Seth found it hard to swallow.

She turned just a bit and leaned into the countertop, about to order a drink from the bartender, when Seth felt the world stop.

Mia.

He almost didn't recognize her. Her lips were glossy, her cheeks had a hint of pink and her eyes had a smoky touch of makeup.

Good god, she looked gorgeous. He'd seen all her features before, admired them even. But with the right dress… the right makeup…it was impossible to ignore that she was stunning. She looked nothing like the mechanic she was all day.

Seth regained his composure, thanking his lucky stars she hadn't noticed his slack jaw or widened eyes.

"Mia," he said, his voice a bit wobbly. He cleared his throat. "You look…wow."

She turned at the sound of his voice, but her expression hardly changed. "Oh. Hey."

He bristled at her lack of reaction. Why was she acting so oddly? Their date a couple of days ago had been amazing. Hadn't she felt the same way?

"How are you?"

She smiled. It was a little cool, a little standoffish.

"Great," she said, taking a swig of the beer the bartender handed her. He couldn't help but notice the bright red polish on her nails. Something about it—about that bright red statement of femininity—made him want to kiss her. Starting with her hands, moving up her arms...

But at this rate, he would be getting nothing but the cold shoulder.

"Good to hear."

She just nodded and took another sip. "I've got to get back to my group. It was nice seeing you," she said, stepping away before he could reel her in. Instead he just nodded, at a loss for words.

She'd left him speechless. He didn't know a woman could do that to him.

As soon as she was out of earshot, Nate ribbed him. "Oh, Mia! Won't you marry me, Mia?" Nate let go of a long, honking laugh, and Seth glowered at him.

"Seriously, dude, that girl has you wrapped around her finger and she doesn't even know it."

Seth let out a long sigh and rubbed his eyes, forcing himself to face the bar despite how much he wanted to turn and get another glimpse of her.

He was in trouble. Oh, was he in trouble.

CHAPTER FIVE

MIA SAT IN A CORNER BOOTH at Andre's, willing herself not to look in the direction of the bar. And yet the longer she tried to ignore it, the harder it became. The only thing she could do each time she felt the nearly-impossible-to-resist urge was take another swig of her beer.

The bottle was empty, but it didn't stop her from doing it anyway. Most of her friends had already gone home, and the rest were busy mingling. She didn't have the desire to do either, because she was too busy staring at *him*.

Seth. She'd hoped he'd be here, of course. Andre's was one of the more popular bars for teams because it was close to the shops and offered specials and discounts for team members. And yet she hadn't mentally prepared herself, hadn't thought of what she'd say if they bumped into each other.

And then she was standing next to him. She saw him mere seconds before he saw her, just enough time to rein in her erratic heartbeat and appear composed. But she'd overdone it, acted aloof and cold, and now there was no way Seth would approach her. She'd acted like their go-kart date had been nothing. So now she had to fix it.

Mia was surrounded by men every day of the week. She talked to them, worked with them and ate lunch with them.

So why was Seth different? Why did he bring out something in her that no one else did?

She couldn't help the surge of happiness at his reaction
to seeing her dolled up. His eyes lit up, those golden flecks
brightening until they nearly glowed. Nor could she stop
the confident swagger as she walked away, hips swinging,
hair tossed over her shoulder. She wanted to turn back and
see if he was watching her. It took everything in her not to.

But now, she could only sit quietly in the corner, watching him mingle and laugh with friends, as she sipped at an
empty bottle.

Why hadn't she said something flirty? Something…

Well, something other than, "I've got to get back to my
group." How foolish! She could have stood next to him,
asked him how he was, congratulated him on his team's
win…but she'd panicked and walked away.

She could get up, order another beer, talk to him again.
But she couldn't drum up the nerve to do it.

Seth was an attractive man, and judging by the attention he was getting, the rest of the women in the room
noticed. Two of them had already spent the past twenty
minutes talking to him. Now, a tall woman with platinum
hair was leaning into his shoulder, laughing.

Seth was so out of her league, it wasn't even funny. Ten
minutes ago, one of them had whipped out her phone, and
though Mia couldn't be sure, it seemed that Seth was giving her his number.

Mia wanted to be the one standing there, her hand casually
placed on his shoulder, leaning in and laughing at his jokes.

The longer she sat in the corner, quietly drinking, the more
she psyched herself out. Was she really this out of practice?

It was those eyes, that crooked little smile… He was impossible to resist. All she had to do was get up and walk over to him. She was dizzy with going in circles, deciding to do it and then changing her mind.

Just when Mia thought she'd spend the rest of the night staring at Seth and arguing with herself, a man walked up and grabbed the chair opposite her, spinning it around and sitting in it backward. He was wearing a black ball cap on backward, a crisp green button-up shirt with a white T-shirt underneath and blue jeans. He was a little shorter than Seth, but probably the same age.

"Hi," he said, flashing her a goofy, arrogant grin. "I'm Nate. Seth's friend."

"Oh. Hi," Mia said, tentative. What did he want?

"I'm going to do you a favor," he said.

"Yeah?"

"Yeah. I'm going to sit here for the thirty seconds it takes Seth to notice I'm talking to you. Then I'm going to leave." He propped his elbows up against the back of the chair, leaning on one arm, looking far too pleased with himself.

Mia just stared, her mouth slightly parted, no words coming to mind. Was he serious? Or was he mocking her? Had he seen her watching Seth all night?

"Why?"

Nate smiled. "Because—"

Before Nate could finish his sentence, a hand clamped down on his shoulder, making Nate wince a little as the grip tightened. Nate's button-up shirt wrinkled between Seth's fingers. Mia looked up to see Seth staring down at Nate, an unreadable expression on his face. "Nate. I see you've met Mia," he said.

Mia wanted to laugh out loud and nearly did. How had Nate known?

More importantly, when could she thank him?

Nate looked over at Mia, winked and then got up from the table, straightening out his rumpled shirt. "Yes. Unfortunately, there is a beer calling my name. I'll leave you to it," he said, then quickly walked away.

Mia stopped fighting the grin and smiled up at Seth. "Your friend fancies himself a matchmaker."

"Either that, or he wanted me to vacate my stool," Seth said, pointing over his shoulder. Nate was now sitting back at the bar, but a redhead had sat down beside him, and Nate was already throwing a casual arm around her shoulders.

Mia shrugged. Did it matter? Nate had made her decision for her, and she was only happy to accept it. "Either way. Have a seat."

Seth turned the chair back around and sat down, moving a coaster so that he could put his mug down on the table.

Mia raised a brow. "Neat freak?"

Seth looked at his drink, and then at the others on the table. None of them were on coasters. He sighed. "You caught me."

"My mother would love you. Every time I'm at her house, she's harping at me about coasters. I don't even own a set."

"Maybe I'll ask her out instead," Seth said, his tone playful.

Mia leaned into the table, wiggling her finger to get Seth closer. "If you really want to impress her," Mia said, whispering into his ear, "she loves a good Sudoku puzzle."

Seth laughed as Mia sat back in her chair. It was so easy to talk with Seth. Flirt with him. Laugh with him. He had such a light, easygoing nature that it made Mia forget to be serious.

A waitress stopped by, and Seth ordered two beers.

Seth put his hand up to silence her. "It's just a drink, Mia."

"I swear, I wasn't going to resist," she said, grinning at him.

"You mean you've decided to surrender yourself to my charms?"

Mia snorted. "Something like that."

She couldn't stop smiling. This was…exactly what she needed. Just five seconds of talking to him, and it was as if every worry in the world had disappeared, and she finally felt like she was only twenty-one.

Maybe it was the beer or three talking, but Mia felt lighter, happier, ready to give in. So this was it: she was waving a white flag, surrendering to whatever it was she had going on with Seth. For this second, she would stop second-guessing it.

Their beers arrived, and Mia felt herself unwinding even further as they sat and talked. It was much easier when she let her guard down, when she stopped trying so hard to be perfect.

"Do you want to dance?"

"Yes," Mia said, so quickly she surprised herself. She didn't dance. Not really. But why not?

She followed him out toward the floor, where a small group of couples were swaying to a country song. She only hesitated a moment before putting her arms around his shoulders as he put his hands on her back.

It was…nice, actually. And not nearly as awkward as she'd expected. In fact, Mia felt comfortable in his arms.

One song bled into another, and she lost track of how long they danced, swaying silently, bodies edging closer and closer. The tension that had crackled between them began to sizzle as Mia moved and swayed, unable to get as close to him as she wanted.

Mia was so much shorter than Seth that she could rest her cheek against his chest.

Seth moved his hand to her face and tipped her chin upward, and before Mia could even close her eyes he pressed his lips into hers.

She snapped her eyes shut and lost herself in the moment, the song fading into the background as Seth let go of her back and put one hand on each side of her face, leaning down farther, kissing her harder.

Mia had to pull away to catch her breath, her chest heaving, the sparkling lights over the floor seemingly spinning around them. Something she hadn't felt in months began to swirl and build inside her, and she couldn't help but wish they were anywhere but a crowded bar.

"Do you want to get out of here?" Seth whispered into her ear, his voice husky.

Mia just nodded, and Seth slid one hand off her back, but kept the other there, guiding her through the crowd and out the door into the cool night air.

It was startling how silent it was outside, only the heavy bass beat reverberating through the night. Mia blinked out of the trance of being in his arms.

But then she ignored the voice in her head—the one that belonged to the tomboy mechanic—and listened to the girl inside, the one ready to break free. He held the door open as she climbed in, and then shut the door. He was at the driver's seat in seconds.

They made their way through the quiet streets outside the bar. A glance at the dashboard clock revealed it was after ten. Mia had spent nearly four hours at Andre's.

Mia's heart stopped completely when they pulled up at Seth's house. He killed the engine and silence engulfed them.

For just one second, she thought about yanking the door open and jumping out. But then his hand found hers.

"Are you sure about this?"

When she looked at him, at his expressive brown eyes, Mia just nodded.

CHAPTER SIX

WHEN SETH AWOKE, the LCD display on his alarm clock read 11:40 p.m. The room was still dark, enshrouded in shadows. For a moment his heart soared, then slammed to the ground. He'd only drifted asleep for a moment. But it was long enough for her to disappear.

She was gone. Her side of the bed was cold, the sheets barely rumpled. How long ago had she snuck out? Did she stay at all? He reached a hand out, his palm smoothing over the silk sheets.

He'd fallen asleep, his arm wrapped around her, his lips curled in an eternal smile. There was just something…*right* about her. Something that drew him in, that made him want to be near her.

It was the fact that everything about her contradicted itself. The innocent way she looked at him, but the wise-beyond-her-years way she approached work. The pure strength and skill of her hands as a mechanic, but the soft curves of her as a woman.

She was different than every other girl. She was…

Everything he'd never known he wanted.

Being with her made him grin so much that his cheeks hurt. But now he frowned as he sat up and rubbed his eyes, straining to hear if there were any noises in the house. Maybe she was just in the bathroom. Maybe she'd…

But the house was silent.

And it shouldn't have bothered him quite so much. On the rare occasions he'd brought a woman to his house, the morning after was always a little awkward. He didn't like the idea of hurting a girl's feelings, of leading her on when he didn't want a relationship. It was a weird balance, showing them out, kissing them good-night—or was it good-morning?—and then shutting the door. Sometimes he'd say "I'll call you," even though he knew he wouldn't.

But he wouldn't have, couldn't have, done that with Mia.

With Mia, he'd only pictured her in his T-shirt, sipping on some coffee while he made breakfast. He wanted her to sit with him, to talk and laugh while he made bacon and eggs and everything he could find, anything to make it so the morning would never end.

What was Mia thinking? Everything had been going perfectly. Lunch, the go-karts, Andre's. Then she came home with him…only to creep out in the middle of the night.

Did she regret it? Or was this about her job and her reputation? Was she really *that* worried about being seen with him?

He felt oddly…empty.

Seth didn't even have her phone number. Or her address.

He didn't have anything but a name.

Maybe he'd put the cart before the horse, but somehow he'd have to fix it.

Because he didn't want *just lunch* or *just a drink* anymore.

Now that he'd had her, he wanted more.

He wanted Mia. Plain and simple.

He could go to the team shop, find Mia, ask her out again and refuse to take no for an answer.

But it would probably backfire. Mia's job was too important to her. And that was something he could understand. If she really left to keep things under wraps, and if he created a scene at her job, it would only prove to her that he didn't understand her, that a relationship with him would interfere with everything she'd worked so hard to earn.

She'd been clear. Her team couldn't know about him. In fact, he wasn't sure how his own team would react, if they knew. But he didn't care, either.

So he'd play it safe. He'd keep an eye out for her at the local hot spots, and if all else failed, he'd have to catch up with her at Martinsville.

Which was still several days away.

Seth fell back into bed and pulled a pillow over his head. The idea of not seeing her for a few days was surprisingly hard to take.

When had he gotten in so deep?

JUST BEFORE MIDNIGHT, Mia sat down at Maudie's, resisting the urge to kick off her high heels. Thank god it was still open, because she needed a place to think. Her toes were aching, and she was still wearing her little black dress. She could've had the taxi take her all the way home, but she'd opted to come to Maudie's instead, for a coffee and some food, before walking the two blocks to her car.

Unlike the usual buzzing lunch hour, the diner was desolate and empty. A gray-haired man with a wiry beard sat by himself in the corner booth, flipping through the newspaper, and two ladies sat at the other end of the long counter, gossiping about what they'd read in the latest tabloids.

The new waitress Sheila had pointed out during Mia's

first lunch with Seth, Mellie, set a menu down in front of her and started filling her mug full of coffee. It must have been obvious she needed it.

"Rough night?" Mellie asked, setting the coffeepot back on the hot plate. She picked up a rag and set to work cleaning up the counter, keeping one eye on Mia.

Mellie just raised an eyebrow and nodded. Though the girl looked barely twenty, she seemed to have a maturity that belied her age. A sort of wise aura about her.

"It was…amazing. And terrifying. I don't know yet."

"Then it must involve a man," she said, smiling a little.

"Yes. That it does."

Mellie picked up the empty coffeepot and filled it with water, setting the machine to make another carafe full.

"I'd offer you advice, but it wouldn't be any good. But I can listen if you need it."

Mia pursed her lips and stared intently at her coffee as she stirred it, even though she hadn't added any sugar or milk. "Just wondering if I can possibly make room for another thing in my life."

Mellie let go of a long, slow sigh. "I hear you there. There's never enough time in the day for everything. Never."

Mia nodded, swallowing the lump in her throat. Being with Seth tonight had awakened something in her, something she'd buried, something she wasn't sure she could bottle back up. And that scared the hell out of her.

One of the two ladies at the end of the counter signaled for Mellie, and the girl walked away to help them.

Mia took a long, scalding drink of her coffee. She normally added sugar and milk, but today called for the strongest thing she could find. Something, anything, to clear her head of the last of the alcoholic haze.

She was alternating between electric, euphoric energy, and pure, raw nerves.

Because she knew already that she wanted to be with him again. She'd left his house barely ten minutes ago, and she already wanted to return.

Tonight had been…the most amazing night of her life. She hadn't felt that sexy, that…feminine…ever.

And she knew she couldn't just return to reality and being one of the guys again. She just had to figure out if she could really pull it off. Balance her work and something with Seth.

If it was casual, no strings attached, it could work. Seth had been okay with keeping their date quiet. And he was the perfect guy for a casual relationship. He wasn't the kind of guy to expect commitment. Commitment was something she couldn't give.

Could it really work? Maybe she didn't have to choose between her job and Seth, as long as it was something with no attachments, no requirements.

Something with no threat to her career.

Finally, she'd have a little fun.

She'd already proven to herself that she could slip out of his bed and walk away, hadn't she?

Mellie had been right when she said there was never enough time in the day.

Because there wasn't, not for Mia. So she'd just save a little bit of her *night* for him instead.

It was too tempting not to try.

Mia smiled to herself as she added a little cream and sugar to her coffee. Martinsville was a tiny track, another half-mile oval, barely big enough for all the teams.

She'd never looked forward to the next race quite so much.

Mellie came back and refilled Mia's coffee. "Doing okay?" she asked, setting a few napkins down in front of Mia with one hand and brushing some stray strands of hair behind her ear with the other. The girl was in perpetual motion, filling, fixing, tidying, scribbling, wiping. It never stopped.

"Yes. I'm…more than okay."

Mia smiled.

She was great. And in another few days, she'd be even better.

CHAPTER SEVEN

BY THE TIME SETH'S TEAM was unloading the car in Martinsville, he was already looking for the No. 483 team, hoping Mia would be hanging around the Sanford hauler, dressed in her well-fitted shop pants and button-up, her hair in its usual tight-and-tidy twist.

He knew that she needed to dress that way. Knew that loose hair and jewelry were both an inconvenience and a danger.

But he would forever picture her as that girl at Andre's, her loose hair just brushing her shoulders, her legs bare, her feet in those delicate little sandals.

Seth liked that she could be both the girl at the shop and the girl in that dress, the one that drove him wild.

Thoughts of her had plagued him for days. Their evening together seemed to play in a constant loop in his mind. If only he'd thought to get her phone number. He had to know what she was thinking. Did she regret what they'd done? Was she thinking about him like he did her?

And when, exactly, had he become so much like a high schooler with a crush? This wasn't him. It was throwing everything off.

Seth tripped over a small rock, barely catching himself before landing on his face. Jeez, at this rate, he was going to wreak havoc with his absentmindedness. He'd probably drop the car before the tire changer got his hand out from underneath it. And then what would they do?

"Smooth," Nate said, chuckling. "Distracted, are we?"

He took in a deep, slow breath, forcing all images of her wild, unruly brown hair out of his mind.

"Not at all."

"Could have fooled me."

Seth glared at his friend. The man was too perceptive for his own good and had a penchant for knowing what Seth wanted before Seth did, whether it was a beer or a break…or an excuse to talk with Mia at the bar.

Maybe he'd have to exercise a little patience with Nate today, as Seth probably would have spent all night watching Mia from afar if Nate hadn't cut in and put the two together.

Nate leaned against the edge of the hauler, studying Seth's face. "So you never did tell me… How was she? Like a tiger, I'm sure."

Seth's blood pounded into his ears and his fists involuntarily clenched. Nate looked down at Seth's hands, caught the change in him and his lips curled into a smile.

"I knew it. I knew it!" Nate said, far too gleeful as he stood upright and gave Seth a good smack on the shoulder.

Seth took a deep steadying breath, trying to force his posture to remain neutral. "I have no idea what you're talking about."

"Like hell you don't. You're *still* thinking about the woman from Andre's… Mia, was it? You haven't been yourself all week." Nate's grin turned a little toothier. "Now granted, she was *pretty* attractive. That dress…those legs…"

"I have no idea what you're talking about," Seth repeated, cutting Nate off.

Nate laughed and clapped a hand on Seth's back. "And here I thought you'd lost your touch. Good to see you back in the game. Though she doesn't quite fit your usual type, does she? And a woman from work? That's a new one. Could be messy."

Seth sighed and rubbed a hand over his forehead, taking one step back so Nate couldn't slug him again.

Playing dumb would get him nowhere. "So I'm a bit distracted."

"No one else has noticed," Nate said, before Seth could voice his concern. "Your secret's safe with me. But if you foul up on the stops, then I'm afraid all's fair."

"Rest assured, I'll be focused."

"Great." Nate started to walk into the hauler, then took a step back. "And Seth?"

"Yes?"

"For god's sake brush your teeth. Did you eat a head of garlic for breakfast?"

Seth's eyes widened, and Nate laughed. "Kidding."

Seth rolled his eyes. Nate had a poor sense of humor.

But just in case, Seth set off in search of a mint.

MIA WASN'T SURE IF SHE was annoyed or overjoyed when she discovered that her team's pit stall was next to Seth's team's. She knew she'd be tempted to watch him instead of her own car. And no doubt the rest of her team didn't like it, not when Seth's team also happened to be Grosso's. Granted, the teams were professional enough to leave one another alone. But it didn't mean they were happy about it.

As a mechanic on the B team, she would only take over when the car was brought back to the garage. Or, as was the case in Martinsville, the hauler.

Watching them work during the most intense moments of the race only served to inspire her further. The team could make changes that would make or break the race. They could fix what wasn't working, could perfect the car until it was the fastest one on the track.

Mia could prepare it, but the A team could perfect it. Someday, she'd wear that uniform, would work out on the track beside the best of the best. For now, seeing them in action was enough to add fuel to the fire that was always burning in Mia.

Unlike Bristol, Martinsville was a little more intimate. Somehow the layout made it feel as if the fans were even closer.

This was Mia's first Martinsville race, though they'd visit the place again before the year was out. Ethan, the crew chief, had agreed to let her sit on the box. For once, Cassie wasn't at the track.

Ethan and Cassie married nearly a year ago, and yet they were still as deeply in love as if they'd been married yesterday. Cassie came to every event she could manage, sitting beside Ethan. Even Ethan's little girl, Sadie, was at the track on occasion. Someday Cassie would, no doubt, give Ethan another child, but Mia couldn't imagine that Cassie would love her own biological child any more than she loved Sadie.

Mia wasn't sure how Cassie managed to watch the race when she almost always had a hand gripping her husband's, when they seemed to constantly exchange secret, longing looks. If anyone else dared to distract Ethan, there would be serious trouble, but for Cassie, he'd do anything.

In fact, Ethan's trouble saying no to Cassie was the very reason Mia had a job. Cassie still thought of Mia as her kid

sister, and when Mia had agreed to play babysitter for
Ethan's daughter instead of getting the mechanic's job
she'd thought she would get, Cassie marched straight over
to the Sanford shop and chewed out Ethan. Next thing Mia
knew, she'd become a full-time intern at the shop, and it
was Cassie watching over Sadie.

It was kind of sickening and kind of endearing, and Mia
couldn't decide which feeling to go with. Ethan was her boss,
and she most definitely didn't see him the way her sister did.

Mia supposed it was good, though, as long as her
sister was happy.

Mia was just glad Cassie wasn't around. Her sister
would notice something was going on between Mia and
Seth. Then Mia would have to explain their relationship,
which was sure to be awkward.

Mia stood in the midst of the rest of the crew, leaning
against a stack of tires. They were discussing the last test
session at Martinsville, and what sort of changes the
weather might make on the car. Mia listened intently. This
was the sort of thing she'd need to have a firm grasp on if
she ever wanted to be part of the A team.

The racing technical program had taught her all about
the mechanics of a car—how each piece worked in unison,
how small changes added up to a big difference. But it
couldn't replace experience. If she paid attention, really
listened to her teammates and soaked up as much knowl-
edge as possible, she'd move up faster.

As they started to talk about the track surface and tire
wear, Mia saw a group of crew members in blue-and-white
uniforms making their way to the No. 414 pit.

And Seth was among them. Towered over them, in fact,
impossible to miss.

It was the first time she'd seen him since she'd left him, his eyes shut as he slept. She'd had to untangle her legs from the sheets, slip out from under his arm. But she couldn't resist kissing him on the cheek as she left, wondering what he was dreaming about as he sighed in his sleep.

The conversation faded around her as she turned to look at him.

Mia wished she was wearing sunglasses so that she could look more openly. Instead she had to settle for a fleeting glance that told her all she needed to know: he looked just as good in his uniform as he had that morning when she'd left, bare beneath the sheets. The suit only served to remind her how broad his shoulders were, how narrow his waist was, how tall he was. His auburn hair and five o'clock shadow had been burned into her memory, and his brown eyes were, to her shock, staring right at her.

Dang it, she blushed, turning away and looking out at the track, even though there weren't any cars on it yet. She could feel Seth's eyes on her as she pretended to be enthralled with the empty racing surface for a minute or two. She waited long enough for Seth to get past her before turning back and listening in on the conversation again.

"You can go relax, you know."

Mia blinked and turned toward the voice of Brian. They hadn't talked much since the day at the shop, when he'd been so sure she needed assistance. Mia had all but decided that she was being overly sensitive. He *was* a good mechanic, after all. She could learn a thing or two from him.

"I'm okay," Mia said. "I gotta learn this stuff somehow if I'm ever going to make the A team."

Brian snorted and then turned away, but not before she caught his smirk.

"Something funny?" she asked, propping one hand up on her hip.

Brian raised one eyebrow, not wiping the smirk from his lips.

"Just that you think you'll ever make the A team."

Mia felt as if she'd been slapped. "Why *wouldn't* I?"

One of the other Sanford mechanics gently pushed on Brian's elbow, as if to cut him off, but Brian just yanked his arm away and crossed them at his chest. He wasn't going anywhere. "You really think you're going to make it out there?" He pointed to pit road.

"Of course. You think I'm here to skate by? I want to be the best. I want to be one of you guys."

Brian laughed and rolled his eyes. "That's where you'll get into trouble." He spun around and started to walk away, then stopped and looked back at her. "Because you'll never be one of us."

And then Brian stalked away.

Mia was so shocked she was frozen in place, staring after him. One of the other team members shouted after Brian and jogged off, but the others just stood there, all of them looking a little off-kilter.

"Don't listen to him," Ernie, another A-team member, said. "Man's not half the mechanic you are."

Mia just nodded, still at a loss for words.

Her team members finally broke away from the group meeting, going to grab bottles of water or sports drinks before their car would start practice.

Mia waited until her anger cooled, until she could finally muster rational thought, and then turned toward the pit box.

And that's when she saw Seth, at the edge of the

Grosso box. He was pretending to be tying his shoe, but when she turned around he looked up, and their eyes met for one long moment.

"He's full of crap and you know it," Seth said, turning back to his shoe, so quiet she was sure no one else could hear him.

"I know," Mia said, walking toward the box, slowly, casually kicking a few rocks.

"I'd like to punch him in the face."

And then Mia couldn't help it. She laughed, the anger and frustration vanishing on the wind.

"Thanks."

And then she met his eyes—just for a second—before reaching for the ladder and climbing up.

This thing she had with him, whatever it was, was worth it.

She made her way to the top of the box, forcing herself not to look back at him until she was secure in her seat.

Seth had his back to her as he stood beside Nate, his friend from the bar. Nate, if she remembered correctly, was a gas man for the No. 414 car.

Mia paused near the ladder to the pit box and met Nate's mischievous blue eyes. He grinned and nodded at her, a subtle move, but enough to make Seth turn around. Based on what Mia knew of Nate, that was exactly what he'd intended to have happen.

Mia forced herself not to take in a sharp breath, instead smiling softly at Seth, her eyes unblinking. He stared back, expressionless for a moment, until his lips edged into the tiniest smirk.

It was as if he knew he had her, that just seeing him made her picture that night, made her wish they could repeat it.

His confidence was both sexy and annoying. Did he

know how attractive he was? Did it come from experience? Maybe women always came around again, wanted another shot at him.

Mia rolled her eyes, and his smirk melted into a full grin, as if he knew exactly what she meant by her gesture. Then she tore her eyes away from him, hoping no one had noticed their exchange.

Shaking her head, she climbed up onto the box.

She'd been right all along. Seth was trouble.

The very best kind of trouble.

HOURS LATER, MIA WAS sweaty, dirty and weary. She'd been wrenching on the blue-and-yellow Sanford car for hours now, despite the fact that they'd qualified a reasonably decent twelfth.

Reasonably decent didn't fit in Ethan Hunt's vocabulary, and neither did it fit in Trey Sanford's.

As all drivers had to be, Trey was competitive. And he and Ethan had put their heads together to create a laundry list of changes that had kept Mia under the car for hours.

Last week's runner-up finish had only added fuel to the fire. Maybe if they'd made one more tweak to the car, Trey would have been the one burning out his tires after the checkered flag. Instead he'd done interview after interview, forced to remain cheerful even through his frustration. It didn't help that it had been Kent Grosso who won, as Trey had a not-quite-friendly rivalry with Seth's driver.

One that went back years. It never quite burnt out, just sort of simmered below the surface. They were civil, professional. But they didn't necessarily like each other.

Trey had been *this close* to his first win of the season.

And a win this early could provide the momentum needed to make his way into the Chase for the NASCAR Sprint Cup, the one thing every driver wanted.

By the time Mia had tightened the last bolt and the car had been fired up again, all she could think about was falling into bed, and she nearly fell asleep during the short ride to the hotel.

Once inside, Mia headed to the front desk to ask for a wake-up call. By the time she was standing in the elevator, she needed to lean against the wall for support.

Just as the doors were closing, a hand shot in between them. When they parted again, a bolt of electric energy turned Mia from sleepy to wide awake.

Seth stepped into the lift. "Hey." He gave her that casual, crooked smile, the one that sent a wave of tingles down her spine.

Mia had to fight the urge to bolt upright. Instead she did her best to play it cool, and just smiled back at him as her stomach twisted.

They hadn't talked much since that night at his place. They hadn't…anything. She'd just watched him from her spot on the pit box, studied him when he didn't know she was looking and tried to come up with a way to talk to him without being noticed by her team.

But at a track as tiny as Martinsville, she hadn't come up with anything.

"How's it going?" Mia had to force herself to stay leaned against the wall, her heartbeat ever increasing.

"Not bad. Long day. You?"

"That's an understatement," she said, gesturing to her dirt- and oil-covered clothing.

"No one can pull off that look quite like you," he said.

His eyes swept over her clothing, slowly, before he reached forward to press the 10 button.

"We're on the same floor," she said. She hadn't even remembered to push the button for her floor, that's how tired she was. She stared at the yellow light on the button, trying to think of something else to say.

She couldn't remember why she'd felt so weary. The air in the elevator seemed to be full of enough adrenaline to fuel her for hours.

"I'm not actually on the tenth floor," he said, turning to look at her. His eyes burned, nearly glowed, as he closed the distance between them. She turned her face upward, stared into his eyes.

Mia took a sharp intake of breath, trying to fill her lungs as her heart beat out of control. She was already against the wall, nowhere else to go, as he leaned down and pressed his lips to hers.

Mia wrapped her arms around his neck as he leaned down, doing his best to make up the height difference between them. Mia stood on tiptoe, kissing him back with everything she had.

He pulled back just a bit, letting his forehead rest against hers, their lips nearly touching as he spoke. "I heard you telling your room number to the front desk," he said. "I'm actually on the twelfth floor."

Then he smiled without pulling his lips away from hers.

The elevator dinged, but neither of them moved.

"Well? Are you coming?" she asked, sliding along the wall, away from him. She put one hand in the doorway to keep it from closing, extending the other out to him.

He reached out and clasped her hand, interweaving their fingers. "I thought you'd never ask."

CHAPTER EIGHT

TWO HOURS LATER, MIA LAY beside Seth, staring at the ceiling. The room was so dark she could barely make out the stained-glass light fixture.

Seth's hand found Mia's, and he intertwined his fingers with hers. It was the only part of them touching, and somehow it made the connection feel stronger, more intimate, even though it was only their palms.

"Do you like all the traveling?" Mia asked. If she wasn't holding his hand right that moment, it would have been like asking the darkness.

"Yes. Would be nice to have more time to explore, but I can't complain. I've seen most of the country over the last few years. A little tough at first, but you'll adjust." His voice was soft, quiet, introspective. "It's sort of crazy, isn't it? One town and then another and another… They sort of bleed together."

Mia nodded, though she wasn't sure Seth could see it. "If anything is worth it, though, it's this."

If Mia didn't know better, she'd swear she could *hear* Seth smile as he gave her hand a little squeeze. "Your passion is inspiring."

She laughed. "Right."

"I'm serious. My buddy pretty much paved the road to

NASCAR for me. But you, you knew you were fighting an uphill battle. And you went for it. You went to school knowing people were going to notice you for all the wrong reasons. And after that, you joined a sport full of men. And you hold your head high."

Mia was thankful it was too dark for him to see her blush.

Seth turned and used his free hand to nudge her face toward him, until her nose brushed his. He kissed her softly on the lips, and then turned back toward the ceiling.

Mia couldn't stop herself from sighing. Being around Seth was quite possibly the only thing that made her unwind, like a tightly coiled spring slowly straightening out. There couldn't possibly be anything *wrong* with a relationship like that, right?

And yet sometimes, in tiny little moments, she still felt a little bit freaked out about her decision to be with Seth.

"I know what you're thinking," he said.

"Oh?"

She hoped he didn't.

"Yeah. You're thinking: where has this guy been all my life? This perfect hunk of burning love?"

Mia laughed and smacked him on the chest. "You're such a dork."

"A dorky hunk of burning love?"

She snorted. "Something like that."

"I just want to be *very* clear on the burning-love part. I can't be misrepresenting myself on my résumé."

"Oh yes, that would be very serious. Where do you think you'll fit the burning-love part? What with your many skills and talents?"

"After the ice-skating part, of course. But before world-class gumshoe."

"Gumshoe?"

"Yeah, you know, like an investigator?"

"Oh, yes, of course. Gumshoe. How could I forget?"

"I'm not sure. Obviously my mad skills are too much for you to remember. Perfectly understandable."

"Yes, what with your astounding résumé and all, how could a girl keep track of it all?"

"Exactly."

Mia smiled into the darkness. If only the night would never end.

BY THE TIME THE GREEN FLAG dropped on race day, Seth had smiled so often Nate was giving him strange looks.

"Seriously, you look demented."

Seth rested a toe against the concrete barrier and stared out at the track, unwilling to look his best friend in the eye.

Besides, he'd just grin again. He couldn't help it. It was either smile to himself or turn and see Mia sitting on the pit stall next to them, and he'd only grin even more if he did that.

It was impossible not to. The past two nights…they'd been even better than the night at his house.

Somehow Mia had let go of her worries and just *been* with him, acted as if nothing existed outside their door.

That day after qualifying, when he caught her in the elevator…

He'd waited for her while she showered—she'd declined his offer of help, despite his rather convincing arguments—fidgeting as if he was about to experience his first time, which was ludicrous. Women didn't make him nervous. Ever.

But for those minutes, he had been, tapping his toe on the carpet, readjusting his position on the edge of the bed, turning the TV on and then off again. He'd never tell Nate that, of course. The man would never let Seth live it down.

But somehow with Mia, he'd wanted it to be perfect. He'd wanted her to give in to him, to let him show her that it didn't have to be all work and no play.

And she'd done it, and when it was over, she hadn't asked him to leave. In fact, he'd lingered longer than he should have before returning to his room to prepare for another day at the track.

Seth already knew he'd never looked at her like a casual fling. He liked her. He *more* than liked her.

"She must really be something," Nate muttered under his breath.

"She is. Trust me, she is."

It took everything in him not to turn and look at her at that very moment. He could tell by the slightly cool way she regarded him around the team that she still wanted their relationship to be a secret. And he had to respect that. She'd established early on that it would be a secret, or there would be no date at all.

It should have been a dream come true, but instead it chafed. He wanted everyone to know she was his. He wanted to hold her hand as they walked together at the track. Instead he was forced to keep his demeanor light, was forced to all but ignore her.

He did it for her, though he loathed it.

Maybe he never should have agreed to keep it a secret. It had seemed simple, before the go-kart date, before this week.

But already, he was changing his mind. It wasn't un-usual for relationships to transpire on—and off—the track. These were the people they worked with day in and day out. It was natural that sparks of one sort or another would fly. Did their relationship really have to stay in the shadows like this?

A voice buzzed in Seth's ear. "Caution's out, Caution's out."

Every thought of Mia flew out the window as Seth and Nate readied themselves for a pit stop. It had only been a dozen laps, but chances were that the lead cars would be coming down pit road. Twelve laps was just enough time to figure out if anything in the car was off. And for the Grosso team, the yellow couldn't have been better—Kent had reported a vibration two laps earlier.

"Four tires, four tires."

Seth nodded to himself. The only way to ensure they fixed the vibration would be to change them all.

Some of the other teams, no doubt, would take just two. Two tires meant saving time on the pit stop, so Seth's team would have to be spot-on in order to keep from losing too many places.

Seth would race around the other side—before his teammates—to lift the car. They'd be there a heartbeat later, yanking the old tires out and swapping them with a new set. Seth would have to drop the car at exactly the right moment, and then run to the left side, jacking it up just a millisecond before the tire changers were ready to yank off the old tires.

It was up to him to drop the car the exact moment the tire change was complete.

It was him who led the stop, him who had to watch everything going on. If someone dropped a lug nut, fouled up on anything, he had to know it. If he dropped the car before the tire was fully installed, the driver would take off.

And then he'd have to come back on the next lap to fix

it. And coming down pit road when the other drivers didn't meant he'd likely go a lap down.

It was all on Seth.

He stood up on the wall as the blue-and-white car rolled toward them.

Just as their crew chief Perry talked the driver down and into the pits, saying, "Three, two, one," Seth leaped off the wall along with the tire changers and carriers and rounded the front fender just as the car slid to a stop. He slid the jack under the car while the changer was firing up the ratchet gun, loosening the first lug nut.

Seth pumped on the jack handle once and the car was up. He leaned over and grabbed the tire and rolled it around the back of the changer, toward the tire carrier, who grabbed the tire as it rolled toward him and sent it toward the wall where someone would catch it.

The air ratchet guns screamed out as they installed the new lug nuts. Seth dropped the car and raced around to the other side, the tire carriers getting into position.

One pump and the car was up again, Seth leaning over to take the old tire from the changer as the carrier pushed the new tire into the waiting hands of the changer. Simultaneously, the gas man emptied the last drops of gas into the car.

A second later, Seth dropped the car and a voice on the radio shouted, "Go, go, go!

Seth held his breath as he watched his car race toward the line. The stop had been flawless, the kind of well-choreographed dance that ensured good track position.

Six other cars beat the No. 414 car to the line, but Seth knew that some had taken two tires.

Not bad. They'd gained two spots on pit road.

He and the other pit members swapped a few high fives. Seth grinned as the adrenaline ebbed.

It was just the first stop of many, but with each successful stop, Seth felt his confidence increase.

Last year, at the pit-crew competition, he'd made a costly mistake. He didn't get the car high enough before he dropped the jack.

He'd cost them the championship.

No one on the team had given him a hard time. They'd been closer to winning than ever before, and they credited Seth's leadership with their close call.

But to Seth, *almost* wasn't good enough. Maybe that's why NASCAR was such a good fit for him—it was a sport where tenths of a second meant everything, and *almost* kept you from Victory Lane.

He was determined to win the pit championship this year, and that meant practice, practice, practice. During the week, he and the team went through drill after drill. Two tires, four tires, wedge adjustments, sway bar adjustments…one after another, until they were weary.

He could jack the car in his sleep at this point. Two tires, four tires, it didn't matter. He knew what he was doing. Four years in NASCAR, and he had it down to a science.

The track went green again, and Seth felt his body start to unwind. When the car was on pit road, every nerve was on high alert. Sometimes the crew chief would make a spur-of-the-moment change to his orders, and they'd have to react quickly. Sometimes it was a result of a wreck on the track—if the yellow flew while they were caught on pit road, it could make a big impact on their track position.

Once the car was on the track, Seth could breathe again.

And once he could breathe, he could think, and once he could think...

Seth glanced over his shoulder at the Sanford Racing pit stall.

Mia was watching him. She stared down from her place atop the box, clad in her usual shop uniform. Her hair was up in a twist, the few escaping tendrils tucked behind her ears.

She nodded almost imperceptibly at him. He nodded back, his helmet bobbing, making his nod not quite as subtle.

"If you could stop staring at her for more than five minutes, we might have a shot at winning this thing."

Seth snapped his attention back to Nate, who was standing beside him.

"Huh?"

"You've spent more time watching Mia than the track. Out of the corner of your eye, though."

Seth sighed and leaned against the wall to get a better look at his friend.

"It's not going to mess up the stops, Nate."

"I know. I saw that firsthand. You're at your best, no doubt about it." Nate put his hands on his hips and stared out at the track, where the leader was flying by, Grosso half a dozen cars back.

"So what's the problem?"

"No problem, I'm just amused, that's all."

"Why?" Seth asked, growing a little annoyed.

"Because I never thought I'd see the day that Seth Richman was wrapped up in a single girl. Surely, somewhere, a pig is flying."

Seth regarded his friend with an expression that was neither hostile nor amused. Why was his relationship with Mia of so much interest to Nate? "Is it really that surprising?"

Nate shrugged. "I've been your wingman for four years, Seth. It really *is* that surprising."

Seth considered this. They'd prowled the bars together almost since Seth's twenty-first birthday. They'd attended weddings of team members and mingled with the guests, gone to team barbecues and left in separate vehicles…

Nate enjoyed the quests, liked the game and the pursuit.

And Seth had, too. To a point. But ever since Mia came along…

He had half a dozen missed calls on his phone and no desire to return them.

It was Mia or no one, and there was no middle ground. He wanted her. All of her.

It made no sense, but Seth wasn't about to question it.

Before Seth could think of a response, a car rumbled toward them. It was the red-and-blue No. 427 car, the one once driven by Kent Grosso. Now, it was driven by Lucky Parrish, who had cut a tire somewhere on the track and was limping his way to his pit stall. The tire was still intact, which meant no need for a caution flag, and the track was still hot with action.

"Let's not talk about Mia, okay?" Seth said. "For the next three or four hours, it's all work."

Nate nodded. "You got it."

Unfortunately, work didn't last three or four hours. Thirty laps later, it came to—literally—a crashing end.

Trey Sanford's car was moving to pass Kent Grosso. And Sanford was an aggressive driver.

Too aggressive. Sixty laps into the race, he didn't need to be pushing so hard to pass. He could have waited, found the right opportunity. Instead he ducked low, at the same time Kent was swinging downward to make the corner. The two cars needed the same piece of track.

The drivers collided. Their cars smashed together, slid up the track, tires screeching, then slammed into the big white safety barrier with a loud bang.

The Sanford car separated from Grosso, spinning around and sliding down the banking as Grosso continued to skid along the white wall, leaving behind a streak of blue paint.

When the cars came to rest, it was clear Kent's day was done. Both cars lay in heaps of twisted sheet metal. Steam and smoke drifted from the blue-and-white No 414 car.

Seth wouldn't be needing his jack any time soon. That car would be leaving the track on the hook of a tow truck, and it would go directly into the garage. Maybe they could salvage it and ride around the track for a bit to pick up some positions, but even from here, that looked doubtful.

Seth looked over at Mia. Her face was downward, her eyebrows crinkled as she studied their car on the screen in front of her. Beside her, Ethan Hunt was standing, shielding his eyes to the sun as he squinted to see the No. 483 car.

Judging from their expressions, it didn't look too hot for the Sanford team, either. Trey and Kent, two good cars out in one swoop. Both of them top-ten material.

Seth's driver, Kent, came onto the headphones. "What's he doing being so aggressive? Way too early for that kind of driving!"

Judging by the banging noise coming through the headphones, Seth could only guess that Kent was slamming his fists into the steering wheel.

Kent Grosso and Trey Sanford's rivalry was one fueled by the fact that their best tracks were the same places, by the fact that they often ended up in first and second, by the fact that they'd tangled a time of two on the track in previous years.

That time, it was a restrictor-plate race, and Trey was blocking Kent, despite the fact that the Grosso car was obviously faster. So Kent bumped him, too close to the corner, sending Trey sliding up the bank and into the wall.

Kent went on to win.

The dispute was fueled by the media, who loved to analyze the drama on the racetrack, twisting every accident into an intentional wreck.

No doubt they were broadcasting Kent's words at that very moment. Seth hoped his driver wouldn't lose his cool. With technology as it was, half the fans in the stand were probably tuned to Kent Grosso's radio frequency—and the other half were likely listening to Trey Sanford.

The cars on the track slowed for the caution flag as the window nets on each car dropped.

Kent Grosso climbed out first, and to Seth's worry, immediately walked toward the Sanford car. Seth couldn't hear what was being said but Kent pointed up the track and was shaking his fist.

Seth groaned. There were probably twenty cameras facing Kent right now, taking in every gesture. The broadcasters, no doubt, were already analyzing his actions, building the feud into a fight of epic proportions.

This would make the ten o'clock news, that's for sure.

"Way to go, Sanford!" one of Seth's teammates called out.

Only he wasn't talking to the driver. He was glaring at the Sanford team in the pit stall next to them.

Nate grabbed the man's shoulder and pushed him toward the garages. "Let's get out of here," he said.

Nothing good would come of the pit crews getting in an argument. Feuds were solved on the track.

Only on the track.

By the time Kent was done with his tantrum, Seth and his teammates were halfway to the garage, ready to put the scene behind them.

Their day was over. Kent's victory last week had already been undone, and momentum was no longer on their side.

Such was racing.

CHAPTER NINE

LESS THAN FORTY-EIGHT hours before the race in Texas, Seth found himself holding Mia, struggling with the idea of letting her go.

She was so small in his arms, so perfect.

He couldn't seem to unwrap himself from her. He should have slid out of bed hours ago, like he'd done every night before.

Instead he just kept watching her sleep, watching her shoulders move as she breathed.

He wanted to turn her toward him, or at least away from the wall, so that he could see her face.

But he couldn't bring himself to do that, either, so he just kept lying there in the darkness, listening to her sleep.

There had been a moment last night when he could have said something. Could have told her he was tired of sneaking around, that he wanted to be with her and let everyone know it.

But his lips seemed to be glued to each other, and the words refused to dislodge.

Seth slid his arm out from underneath Mia, then froze as she took a sharp intake of breath. By the time he was sitting upright, her eyes fluttered open.

"Go back to sleep," he whispered, leaning over and kissing her on the forehead. "It's almost dawn."

And I haven't slept yet, he almost added.

She nodded, but her eyes didn't shut. She just watched him as he slid off the bed.

"Do you have to go?" she asked, her voice hardly above a whisper.

Was she serious? Did she want a real answer?

Because no, he didn't *have* to go.

He looked over at her, and his heart fell a little. By the sleepy, halfhearted way she looked at him, it was obviously a rhetorical question. She was already grabbing a pillow, snuggling up to it to fill his spot on the bed.

"You know that's how this works. Unless you want your team to know you're fooling around with the enemy," he said, leaning over to kiss her on the temple.

She closed her eyes and nodded, already half-lost in a dream.

Seth stood and watched her for a long moment, aching to climb back into bed with her. But then he just found his shoes and headed to the door.

This was what she wanted.

This was what he *had* wanted.

Not anymore.

MIA'S EYES opened as the hotel room door clicked shut.

You know that's how this works.

They were *fooling around.*

Of course that's how he saw it. That's how he was *supposed* to see it. And that's how she was supposed to feel, too.

Yet somehow she'd been so close to telling him to stay, so close to telling him she didn't care what the team thought anymore.

And that was wrong. Wrong, wrong, wrong.

Mia sat up in bed and rubbed her eyes.

It had taken her nearly an hour to fall asleep.

For the past two weeks, life had taken an insane, frenzied, crazy turn. She and Seth had reached some kind of unspoken agreement. Every night, he tapped on her door, and she ushered him in. They hardly made it ten feet inside the door before he was pulling her shirt over her head…before they were…

Mia blushed and stared down at the burgundy swirls on the quilt.

What she had with Seth was…unforgettable. Amazing.

The highlight of her day.

Oh, who was she kidding? It was more than just the highlight of the day.

It was the highlight of her life.

All she thought about, every second she wasn't with him, was him. What he was doing, what he was thinking.

Whether he thought of her when they weren't together.

And the more she thought of him, the more worried she became. What if she lost her focus? What if she liked being the woman she was with him so much, she didn't want to be a mechanic anymore?

This was the first time Mia had opened herself up to a guy in years. Maybe ever. And now she'd put herself in a precarious position.

It was terrifying. She was afraid to admit that she wanted more and might lose what she had.

Last night, she'd almost admitted it to him. Told him she was starting to want more. She'd been lying in his arms, listening to him breathe. He was snuggled up to her, his face in her hair.

How could something like that be wrong? Maybe it could work; maybe they could be together and let everyone see it and nothing would fall apart because of it.

But even as the words sat on the tip of her tongue, all she did was stare at the drywall, blinking in the dark, her heart aching.

It's just sex, Mia.

She could practically hear him say it. Could see the look on his face as he tried to let her down easy, as he told her that he didn't feel anything for her beyond, well, attraction.

Why'd she have to go and start falling for him? She should have been happy with what they had.

It was that stupid crooked smile, the way he made her laugh, the way he made her feel feminine in a way no one else could. Without him, she was just another mechanic, a girl lost in shop clothes and ponytails.

And she went and ruined it by picturing a life with him that lasted past dawn.

But Seth didn't want that. As sure as she knew anything, she knew Seth didn't do relationships.

Mia put her bare feet down on the carpeted floor and walked into the bathroom, where she turned the water up as high and as hot as she could tolerate before getting in.

But no matter what she did, she couldn't wash away her feelings for him.

CHAPTER TEN

MIA SAT ATOP THE PIT BOX at the Texas race and watched, miserable, as Trey's car headed toward the pit once again.

It was the fourth stop in the last thirty laps of the race. But even with three previous chances, the team hadn't figured out what was wrong. They had mere seconds with the hood up to try a number of options, eliminating one problem after another. Then they'd drop the hood and send the car back out to avoid going yet another lap down.

But something in the engine was still off. For a handful of laps, things would be right again, and they would maintain position. But soon, the car would be dropping, unable to maintain the pace. It didn't sound right, didn't accelerate right.

If they didn't fix it soon, they'd be lucky to stay in the top forty. They'd already be dead last if there hadn't been a wreck early on. With last week's DNF…the season for the No. 483 car was in a backward slide.

Mia stood up as the car slid to a stop and the hood went up. She gripped the edge of the box and leaned over, trying to get a better look. Four mechanics in the blue-and-yellow Sanford Racing uniforms set to work, yanking off the plug wires. They were huddled so closely together it was difficult to see anything.

Mia clenched her teeth. They were changing the spark plugs this time around. At the first stop, they checked for loose wires. At the last stop, they changed the carburetor.

Her fingers itched to be one of them, to be on the A team and get her hands on the car. They had to figure it out. They had to fix it.

Mia watched them as wrenches and hands flew everywhere, lightning quick. It was torture, sitting up on the box, her hands tied, her mind wandering.

She'd done her job well, and they'd qualified in the top five, with a solid car. And the track conditions were similar to the final practice session, when they'd been one of the fastest cars on the track.

So what had happened between then and now?

The team finished changing the spark plugs and dropped the hood, shoving the pins into place before sending it back onto the track.

Their engine packages were good; some of the best of the field. She knew she hadn't made any mistakes, hadn't been careless or sloppy. She'd never do that.

"Do you think it could be water in the fuel?" Mia asked, watching as their car sped up, trying to avoid going another lap down by beating the leaders who were coming down the frontstretch.

Ethan moved one side of his headset off his ear and leaned toward Mia. "Maybe. Nothing we can do about that at this point. Makes sense, though. Definitely crossed my mind."

Mia nodded. Water in the fuel was unusual. And the weather had been dry, which made the introduction of water all the more strange—and unlikely.

But with the car acting like it was—sometimes running fine, other moments bogging down—it was a distinct possibility. Especially since it seemed that changing the plugs hadn't helped, at least not for more than a lap or two. The car was struggling to keep on pace.

Four laps later, NASCAR called them in for being too slow. They were a hindrance to the cars on the track.

Mia sunk into her chair and groaned.

Two races in a row. It was one thing if the action on the track was unavoidable, if a mistake was made or a tire blown, but to be wrecked—possibly intentionally—in one and plagued by problems in another...

It wasn't acceptable.

Not to Mia, not to Ethan, not to the rest of the team.

They were going to be frustrated. Every one of them. The ride home that night in the team's airplane would be quiet at best, filled with grumbles and cusswords at worst. Every one of them hated to lose, and when it fell on them— the mechanics—it was that much harder to swallow.

They couldn't blame another team. They could only blame themselves.

Mia climbed down off the box. The action on the track was still hot, but no one on the Sanford team was thinking about it. The cars raced on, the sounds steadily dimming in her ears.

Mia walked away from the track. Today was a miserable day. She just wanted it to be over.

The team hustled back to the garage as the Sanford car rumbled through the opening on pit road. They were already off the pace, but maybe they could fix it in time to try and get back out there—maybe it could still end up being something simple, obvious and quick. If it took more than a few minutes, though, the day was done. They wouldn't be able to pick up enough positions to warrant getting back out there, not unless someone wrecked out soon.

By the time Mia made it to the garage, the team had the hood up and was surveying the engine, this time with a little more care and time. Their driver, Trey, sat in the driver's seat in silence, his gear still on. Ethan leaned into the netted window, asking Trey a few questions about the handling.

Mia stood near the edges, knowing there wasn't enough room for another set of hands. But even with twenty minutes time, there was no answer. Trey had already given up, dropping his window net and removing his helmet, preparing to concede defeat and climb out.

"Check the fuel," Ethan said, some time later. "It's the only option left."

Brian immediately set to work draining the fuel cell.

And, moments later, it was clear by his expression that he didn't like what he saw. Mia wanted to step forward and crowd around. Her fingers itched to be part of the action, to do *something,* but she forced her feet to stay rooted where she was. There wasn't room for her.

This was how it would feel if she ever got fired. She'd have to sit on the outskirts, watching, aching to be a part of it.

"Mia was right," Ethan said, turning to look at her. "Water in the fuel."

That meant there was no point in going back out. They'd have to totally rework the engine, swap out the fuel lines…

"*Mia* was right?" Brian turned to look at her. "*You* knew?"

Mia narrowed her eyes. What was with the sharp tone in his voice? Was he angry that she'd been the one to figure it out? It wasn't as if Ethan hadn't already thought of the same thing. The other mechanics probably had, too.

Mia and Brian hardly spoke these days. She'd avoided him.

But today, his words seemed to barely conceal his contempt for her. "We'd eliminated most of the options," she said. What was he getting at? "You know the same thing occurred to you."

"Yeah? And the Grosso team had nothing to do with your little idea?" Brian said, giving Mia a pointed look.

Her stomach twisted uncomfortably. "What are you talking about?"

"*You're* the one sleeping with the enemy. You tell me."

Mia stepped back, shocked by Brian's statement. He *knew?* How had he found out? Did he see Seth coming out of her room? How stupid had she been? Had they all known?

If they didn't before, well, they did now. Every member of the team was staring at her. Brian had pulled the rug out from underneath her feet.

But even worse than outing her relationship…was he saying someone had *put* water in the fuel? And that her relationship with Seth had something to do with it? How could he call her out like this, in front of the team?

"Brian, go cool off," Ethan said, his voice gruff.

"What? I saw him—"

"Go," Ethan said, a little louder this time. "Come back when you're thinking clearly."

Mia felt a little shaken at the odd, abrupt twist of events. She backed up to the corner and found a stool to sit on, her head spinning. For Brian to even *suspect,* let alone voice, such a ludicrous idea such as the Grosso team outright sabotaging Sanford…it was ridiculous. And to act as if Mia might have known—or even assisted—in sabotaging her own car?

Totally preposterous. Sure, Kent and Trey had a rivalry that was legendary in the garages, not to mention on the sports networks. Every move they made was dissected, shown in side-by-side video. But the dispute was solved on the track.

They raced, and they raced clean. A bump here and there, maybe, but they wouldn't go this far. Not Kent, not Trey.

Even so, Mia became hyperaware of every glance her way. They all knew now that she'd been seeing someone on the Grosso team. Maybe they'd always known.

Maybe Mia wasn't as clever as she'd thought.

She'd really made of mess of this.

The team wouldn't buy the ridiculous sabotage story from Brian, would they? They couldn't. Sabotage was serious, and while water in the fuel didn't quite make sense, it made even less to think that someone put it there deliberately.

"We need to talk," Ethan said, a few moments later.

Mia's already tense stomach twisted painfully as she nodded and followed Ethan out of the garage and over to the hauler. She stared at the Greenstone Garden Center logo on the back of his team shirt as she walked behind him.

Ethan turned to face her once they were alone in the hauler. His eyes were unreadable. Was she in trouble? Was he concerned? "I'll ask this once, and that's it. Do you have any reason to think the water in the fuel was deliberate?"

Mia just gaped at him. Ethan couldn't be taking Brian's allegations seriously, could he? She shook her head so fast it nearly made her dizzy. "No, I—"

Ethan put a hand up to silence her. "That's all I need. We have no reason to believe it was sabotage. Brian is over-reacting. He's just frustrated by the day. He knows it was up to him and the others to figure out the problem, and he failed. Plus, he wants a win as much as the rest of us."

Mia nodded. "Thanks. I'm glad you trust me."

Ethan nodded and sat down, gesturing to Mia to do the same. "I like you, Mia. Not just as my sister-in-law. You're a strong mechanic. You've proven you've got what it takes.

Brian is just threatened. A few months back, he was on a bit of thin ice—calling in sick too much, doing sloppy work—and I wrote him up. And then you were hired full-time because you're good at what you do.

"Technically, we didn't need another mechanic. I suppose he thought I'd signed you on in order to replace him, and every time you get a little more efficient, he thinks he's that much closer to getting the boot."

Mia remembered how defensive he'd become when Mia said she wanted to be on the A team.

Now it made sense. He thought if she was on the A team, he wasn't.

Ethan rubbed his hands together. "Maybe I let him think that, because it seemed to light a fire under him. Sorry if he made things uncomfortable for you. That didn't occur to me. I'll set him straight."

Mia nodded, relief flooding through her. "Thanks."

Ethan stood up. "Hey, I may have given you a chance because of your sister, but I hired you full-time because you're a damn-good mechanic. Keep it up," he said, then gave her a nod and moved to leave the hauler. Mia stared at the toe of her scuffed black shoes.

Today had taken an unusual, uncomfortable twist.

"Oh, and Mia?"

Mia glanced up to realize that Ethan hadn't left yet. "Yeah?"

"What you do in your personal life is your business. No one else's."

Mia nodded, and Ethan disappeared from the hauler. Mia made no move to get up. She wasn't ready to face anyone.

Brian was jealous and petty. He'd thrown out the sabotage idea with no proof. But even though Ethan had dismissed Brian's allegations, Mia couldn't get rid of the uneasy feeling in her stomach.

Seth wasn't the kind of guy to play dirty. He was honest, sincere, a real person.

Mia leaned back against the wall of the hauler, not quite ready to go back out and talk to her teammates.

Ever since that day Seth sat down in front of her at Maudie's, everything had been topsy-turvy and upside down. It was as if life were accelerating at a faster pace than she could keep up with. She was becoming someone else, someone miles away from the woman he'd sat down across from.

Three weeks ago. That's all it had been. And look how much she'd changed in that short of a time span.

Just imagine if she stayed with him! Where would she be in three *months?* Could her career survive such a transformation?

Why couldn't he have sat down across from someone else?

And why, when he could have a woman who looked like a model, had he sat down with a five-foot-seven mousy-haired girl in a shop uniform?

She'd gone two years almost entirely unnoticed by the guys around her. And then Seth had walked into the res-taurant, locked eyes with her and homed in as if he was on a one-man mission.

No, *mission* was the wrong word, wasn't it? Seth hadn't been out for anything. It had been pure chance and attrac-tion that brought them together.

But Mia couldn't get the voice out of her head—the one that said no sane guy would choose her over a woman who could walk down the runway.

Could Seth have been after her in order to gain an edge for Kent Grosso?

Mia couldn't quite believe it. Seth wouldn't do that. But she couldn't fight the nagging suspicions, either.

CHAPTER ELEVEN

BY THE TIME MIA ARRIVED at Seth's house on Tuesday, he was feeling a little uneasy. She'd stopped by the team shop looking for him earlier that day, and Nate had taken the liberty of giving her Seth's phone number.

When Seth had answered his cell and found her on the other end, he'd been overjoyed. The fact that she'd gone to *his* team's shop had to mean something. Was she ready to go public with their relationship?

But her voice had been…strained. Something was off. He'd spent all day second-guessing everything he'd ever said to her, everything he'd ever done.

Everything *they'd* done.

She hadn't talked to him on Sunday. Their pit boxes might as well have been miles apart, and the Sanford car had retired early. Seth hadn't seen her in three days.

But things had been perfect between them before the race. Each night, he would wait in the hotel bar for a glimpse of her, then, ten minutes later, head up to her room. They made love, and then hours later he had to force himself to leave before dawn.

He couldn't do it anymore. He didn't want to leave her bed when it was over, he wanted to stay with her. And tonight, he'd finally tell her. He'd ask her for more. He didn't want to go to another track in another city and play the same old game.

He wanted to knock on her hotel-room door and not have to worry about someone seeing him do it. He wanted to have an actual conversation with her at the track, instead of watching her from afar.

He wanted to take her on a *real* date, where someone would see them, know that she was his.

She'd simply have to agree. Would that be so bad? To be seen with him, to just *be* with him?

It couldn't be. Not when it felt so right.

By the time Seth was swinging open his front entry, he was ready to sweep Mia off her feet, whether she was ready or not.

It was now or never. He just prayed she'd choose now.

"Hey," he said, leaning down to hug her. She wore a simple flowing blue dress, with strappy flat sandals, making the difference between their heights even greater. She smelled like vanilla and lavender. "You look beautiful."

He couldn't resist picking her up, swinging her around and setting her down inside the tiled entryway.

She giggled softly as he kissed her neck and nibbled on her ear. But she also leaned away from him, bending backward. He didn't want to let her go. Instead he only wrapped his arms tighter around her.

"Seriously," she said nearly out of breath, "stop. I can hardly breathe."

Something wasn't right. She was different tonight. There was an edge about her, about the guarded way she was looking at him.

A wall had gone up.

Seth reluctantly released her, then shut the front door. "You look great."

She looked down at her dress, fiddling with the strings on the halter top. He liked that he had that effect on her, even after he'd seen every inch of her. How could she still be so shy in front of him? "Thank you," she said. But she made no move to slip off her sandals, no move to walk farther into the house.

He reached for her hand to lead her into the kitchen, where he hoped to give her a night she'd never forget. But she stood her ground, and he stopped.

Why wasn't she leaving the entry? Why was she standing near the door?

Her hand went still in his.

"I have to ask you something."

She took in a deep, ragged breath of air. Seth's pulse pounded in his ears.

"What?"

"Did you touch Trey Sanford's car last Sunday?"

Seth's jaw dropped, and he released Mia's hand as he took a large step away from her. It was as if he'd been slapped. The distance between them might as well have been as wide as the Grand Canyon. "Why would you ask that?"

She looked up at him, her expression changing, morphing, and yet he still couldn't read it. "I don't know. God, it was stupid. I knew you didn't do it, but—"

"But you asked anyway?"

She had doubted him. Doubted the very thing that he'd thought they had in common: a mutual passion for doing their jobs, and doing them well.

And she thought he'd stoop as low as to sabotage another team?

Her team, no less?

How could she have thought that? About *him?*

And here he'd thought they were made for each other. Thought maybe, somewhere, she felt the same for him as he did for her.

But he would never, not in a thousand years, think that she could sabotage another team, and the fact that she didn't have the same trust in him…

She stepped forward. "I'm sorry. Obviously you didn't do that. It was stupid of me to say anything."

"And yet you did," he said, his voice a little gruff.

She blinked, staring at the ground, and nodded. "The whole team knows about us. It was another team member who planted the thought in my head, and I couldn't get it out. The way you sat down across from me that day at Maudie's, the way you looked for me, constantly crossed my path, it just seemed like—"

"It seemed like what? That I was plotting for weeks to sabotage your car? Does that really make sense?" Seth stepped toward her, shaking his head, his lips pursed to keep the angry words from flowing out. "It didn't occur to you that maybe I was falling for you?"

Her mouth hung open. She seemed to have no words to say.

This wasn't what it was supposed to be like. This wasn't how he'd planned on telling her.

How could she ever think that he was a cheater? He'd be banned from NASCAR for life.

He stepped forward, grabbed her hand and pulled her into the dining room. Her sandals slapped against the tiles as she hurried after him, trying to keep pace with his much longer strides.

A dozen roses were arranged in a vase on the countertop. Candles littered the dining-room table, and a bottle of champagne had been uncorked, now resting in a bucket of ice. He'd set out plates and silverware and real linen napkins.

And God help him, he'd actually tried to cook for her. Just looking at everything he'd done for her made his heart only twist harder.

He was going to give her everything, and she'd thought he was using her to get ahead in a race.

She'd thought he would *sleep* with her just so he could get close enough to the car to sabotage it.

That is who she thought he was.

And it burned.

Even so, he still wanted her and what they had together, mistakes and all, in front of God and everybody.

"This is what you are to me," he said, gesturing to the table. "Not a way to get ahead. Not some *strategy.*"

When she looked at him, he couldn't figure out what she was thinking. Her voice was flat, unemotional. "I don't know what to say."

"Say you trust me. Say you don't believe I would cheat. Say we can stop running around like there's something wrong with being together."

She bit her lip and looked down at her hands, twisting them together.

"I'm tired of hiding," he said. "I want to be with you."

She sighed and shoved her hands into her pockets. "I know, but my job—"

Seth stepped toward Mia, putting one hand on each shoulder. "It's an excuse. You *know* it's an excuse. Everyone in this business has a personal life. Stop hiding behind your job."

He touched a finger to her chin and lifted her face, to look her in the eye. "I won't keep doing this. It's all or nothing."

When she looked up at him, she was shaking her head, her eyes shimmering. "Then it's nothing. I can't give you more." She stepped back, forcing him to break contact. "Don't you get it? Sometimes when I'm with you I feel like I could blow it all off. Like I'd rather stay with you than go to the shop! I can't risk everything for you. I won't."

And then she turned and walked out of the kitchen.

Whatever he thought they'd had, he was wrong.

Because Mia Connors didn't feel the same way.

CHAPTER TWELVE

By THE TIME MIA WALKED into the shop at Sanford, she looked like an extra from *Night of the Living Dead*.

And she felt like one, too. Her nose was stuffed up, her eyes were puffy and her throat was raw from crying.

She'd screwed everything up in one quick swoop. First, she'd voiced Brian's idiotic conspiracy theory aloud, as if it had merit. If she wanted a way to push Seth away, well, she'd found one. She'd questioned the one thing that meant everything to him.

And if he'd done that to her—if he'd acted as if she were a bad mechanic, or worse, that she wanted so much to win that she'd ruin Kent Grosso's car—she would have been incredibly insulted.

Then, when Seth had asked for a commitment, she'd freaked out and left.

She wasn't ready to give him more. Ever since he came along, everything was changing. She was dressing differently and acting differently, and she wasn't sure she could be everything and do everything without something falling apart.

What if she just kept changing? What if she forgot everything she'd worked for?

She couldn't just *be* with him. It wasn't simple like that.

But now she was miserable. As hard as she'd worked to convince herself that she didn't need him, that she was happy with her job as her sole focus, it was a lie. Because the second she'd walked out of his house, she'd regretted it.

Her heart ached as she thought of the table he'd set for them. Thought of the candles, the roses, the champagne.

He'd cooked, too. And she knew he didn't do that, not for himself. He'd done it for her.

She wanted to go back home, crawl into bed and resume crying.

Instead, she walked to her toolbox and started to ready herself for another grueling day at the shop. She picked up her gloves and a few tools, and headed toward Trey's Talladega car, the one she'd been working on last week. Maybe if she buried herself in work, she could forget about Seth.

At least, she'd planned on it, until a voice crackled over the intercom, asking her to go to Ethan's office.

She sighed and set down a crescent wrench and ripped off her gloves. Every bone in her body was on autopilot as her legs ascended the concrete steps and carried her to Ethan's door, and she sat down in one of the leather chairs opposite his desk.

Ethan looked up from his flat-screen monitor and regarded Mia for a long moment. No doubt he was wondering precisely which truck had run her over.

Instead he just held out a box of tissues.

"Wanted to let you know that another team had fuel problems on Sunday. Looks like our source was bad. It obviously wasn't sabotage."

"Yeah. I know," Mia said, her voice rough. "I knew it all along."

And it was true. She *had* known. So why had she sabotaged her own relationship and asked Seth that?

Why had she let her raging insecurities make her think that Seth couldn't possibly like her for her, that he had to have some kind of ulterior motive?

Ethan looked up at her, his eyes narrowing a bit as he took in her appearance. "Take the day off and sort everything out."

"Am I in trouble?" she asked, her voice rising an octave.

"No. You haven't taken so much as an extra *hour* off since you started. Use the time, come back tomorrow in a better mind-set."

Mia nodded and stood up to leave.

"And Mia?"

Mia paused in the doorway.

"Don't tell your sister I'm going soft," he said, smiling at her. She just smiled back, just a little, and then nodded and left him.

MIA SAT IN HER CAR a few blocks away from the Sanford shop, underneath the shade of a big sycamore, staring at her death grip on the steering wheel.

It took everything she had not to burst into tears all over again.

There had to be a way she could fix this. She'd spent the past hour berating herself and her stupid fears.

Maybe being with Seth would put a little strain on her job. But being without him would be worse. She was a mess without him.

Why had it taken her so long to figure out how she felt about him? Why had it taken so long for her to *allow* herself to fall for him?

She loved her job. But Seth woke up something inside her, and there was no way to go back. No way to undo it.

She had to do something to get him back. She couldn't let him slip away. She had to know what it would be like to walk around, her hand in his. She had to know how it would feel to walk up to him and kiss him in public.

She needed him.

And maybe, underneath all of her stupid excuses, that was what she was actually afraid of.

In all her life, she'd never needed someone. She was the one who worked her way through tech school, the one who proved herself day in and day out, the one who got her own apartment and balanced her own checkbook.

And now she needed someone, relied on him, couldn't tolerate the idea of life without him.

Maybe it wasn't too late. If he really was falling for her, he wouldn't be able to just forget her, would he? If she could somehow prove to him that she wanted him—all of him—maybe he'd give her a second chance.

She could prove to him that she was ready for him, that he meant everything to her.

Maybe if she went to his shop, just walked right in there and talked to him, it would show him that she wasn't who she'd been before. She was willing to let everyone at Cargill-Grosso Racing know that she loved him if it meant he'd reconsider.

It could work. She could go out on a limb, stand in front of everyone, tell Seth how she felt. If she was willing to publicly grovel…he would know that she meant it.

It was the only way to prove to him that she knew she was wrong.

She prayed it worked.

FIFTEEN MINUTES LATER, Mia marched into Cargill-Grosso Racing, still clad in her Sanford Racing shop uniform. The men around her regarded her with cool suspicion. She was willing to bet a Sanford team member hadn't been in the shop in years, if ever.

"Where's Seth?"

Maybe her reputation preceded her, but no one bothered to ask her name—they simply pointed to a side door, and then went back to work.

Mia stalked toward the steel door, yanking it open. If she paused, hesitated even the slightest bit, she would start to doubt this. And it was now or never.

Outside, the entire pit crew was assembled, working through a few drills. Seth stood head-and-shoulders taller than the rest of them, one hand on his jack handle. He was talking with his hands, pointing to the car off and on, commanding the team like a true leader.

When he turned slightly, he caught sight of her, and he went still.

Mia couldn't get her feet to propel her any farther forward, couldn't seem to close the distance between them. She was frozen, her shoes stuck to the concrete.

They were just twenty feet apart, and yet it seemed so far. The longer Seth stared at her, the more of his teammates seemed to notice her, until all of them were just standing there, waiting.

Waiting for her to say something.

"I was stupid," she said, her voice coming out in a hoarse whisper. "I panicked. I knew I was falling for you and I didn't know what that would mean for me. I didn't know how to handle it and fit you in between everything else and I freaked out. You just really caught me off guard because I thought you didn't see me that way. Women like you, you know? I wasn't prepared for you to lay it all out like that. You broadsided me."

Mia swallowed the growing lump in her throat and blinked away the impending tears. "Sabotage didn't make sense. It never did. It was just me freaking out about the whole team knowing about us."

The entire Grosso pit crew seemed to be frozen, listening as Mia poured out every emotion that had been building inside of her for weeks. If she wanted Seth to believe her, she'd have to do it this way—in front of everyone.

Mia paused and closed her eyes. She took in a deep, calming breath, and then closed the distance between them, so that her toes were nearly touching his. "I've gotten used to being invisible. And I didn't think it was really possible that you were seeing me. It was easier for me to believe that you had another reason, that you weren't really into me, but were after something else. I'm sorry I doubted you, I'm sorry—"

Before Mia could finish her sentence, Seth stepped forward and wrapped his arms around her back and yanked her forward, until their lips crashed together and the air disappeared from her lungs.

He picked her up, her toes leaving the ground as he kissed her with more possessiveness than he'd ever shown before. And when it was done, she was breathless, her heart beating out an erratic, crazy pattern.

"You can shut up now," he said, his lips still touching hers.

"You can put me down now," she said.

"Never."

And then she smiled. Because she was sure she never wanted to let him go.

* * * * *

Lady's Choice

Marisa Carroll

CHAPTER ONE

KELSEY KENDALL braced herself against the impact of the gale-force wind that nearly lifted her off her feet. It felt as if she'd just stuck her head out of the window of her race car on the straightaway at Talladega. Except she was in Tennessee, at the famed Bristol short track, and the force of the wind was mechanical, not produced by a speeding race car.

"Kelsey. Baby. The camera loves you. Your fans love you. I love you. The hands on your hips works—hot. Hot. Hot!" Delroy Preston, celebrity photographer, fanned himself with his free hand. "But believe me when I tell you that expression on your face is not sexy," the slender, black-clad figure complained as Kelsey stepped out of the blast of the huge industrial fan that a pair of Delroy's flunkies had commandeered from the PDQ Racing hauler moments before.

"Of course it's not sexy," she said, filtering the annoyance she felt at this whole enterprise out of her voice with a skill developed from years of practice. There were nearly a hundred fans standing around, watching the photo shoot. She never lost her temper around her fans. "Getting blown off your feet onto your backside is never sexy." She ignored the stifled laugher from her teammates assembled beneath the upraised back wall of the hauler as the flamboyant photographer threw up his hands and came stalking toward her. Delroy was only an inch or two taller than her own five feet five inches, with a baby face and an ego that knew no bounds. Kelsey stood her ground. It took more than a mercurial photographer to make her back down from a confrontation. A lot more.

"You always look good to me, Kelsey," a fan hollered from beyond the barricade Security had set up to give Delroy as much room to work his magic as the crowded Bristol infield allowed.

"Thanks," Kelsey yelled back and waved, giving the fan a smile.

"That's what I want. That's what my camera wants. That smile," Delroy begged. "With that smile, you'd look good even if you were wearing a burlap bag." A couple of whistles and a scattering of applause said her male fans, at least, thought so, too. "We could bring down mountains with you in a bikini," Delroy said slyly so that only she could hear.

Kelsey held up her hands in a restraining gesture. It had been this way when she raced on the open-wheel circuit, too. No matter how well she did, how many races she won, her sex—not her driving ability—was always the top priority when it came to marketing her. Shelley Green, the only other female driver in the NASCAR Sprint Cup Series, didn't have to put up with this kind of silliness. But Shelley had worked her way up through the ranks of NASCAR, racing dirt tracks, then NASCAR Nationwide Series cars before landing a ride in the show. Shelley didn't have to prove herself in stock-car racing. Kelsey did. "Check my contract. It says no bathing suits." Her team owner, Jim Latimer, as conscious of the need of publicity in this day and age as she was, nevertheless agreed she could draw the line at a swimsuit spread. "I'm a race-car driver, not a bathing-suit model. Do you make the male drivers you photograph jump through hoops this way?" Knowing Delroy, she thought with a sigh, he probably did.

Delroy opened his mouth as if to confirm what she'd just been thinking when a tall, commanding figure, dressed in the same dark-green-and-medium-blue uniform as Kelsey was wearing, emerged from the interior of the eighteen-wheeler that served as both hauler and garage for the short-track weekend, and headed in their direction. It was her crew chief, Dane Guthrie.

"Kelsey, don't forget we're meeting with the boss in an hour," he reminded her in his habitual gruff, no-nonsense tone of voice.

"I'll be there," Kelsey assured her skeptical-looking crew chief, as two more of Delroy's entourage of assistants bracketed her on both sides and began to fuss with her hair, tweaking the long, sun-streaked blond mass back into some kind of order. "You heard the man. Let's wrap this up. Our team owner doesn't like being kept waiting."

"You can't possibly believe we'll be finished here in an hour?" Delroy fumed. "The light is atrocious. We'll need at least three more hours until we can get the back-lighting I need."

Dane crossed his arms over his chest and lowered his head to give the smaller man a long, hard look. Her crew chief was all business all the time. Like the rest of PDQ Racing, he knew publicity brought in sponsor dollars, but racing still came first with him. "You have one hour. If you want to hang around until after our meeting with Mr. Latimer is over and take some more shots of Kelsey, that's up to the two of you."

Delroy's lower lip protruded in a decided pout. "I am a very busy man, also."

"So we understand each other, right?" Dane replied, his voice hardening slightly.

Delroy looked as if he wanted to argue the point, but thought better of it. "Very well, I will accomplish the impossible and be finished with our so beautiful Kelsey in one hour. But only because my camera loves her so much. She's a natural. You'll see. We'll get the cover shot for the spring issue of *American Sports*. She'll be on every newsstand in the country. On every TV show—network and cable. I guarantee it. I'll make her a star."

Kelsey didn't want to be a star. She wanted to be a NASCAR Sprint Cup Series champion—had wanted it for twenty years, ever since her dad had taken her to her first NASCAR race at the age of six.

Dane glanced at his watch, unimpressed. "Now you've got fifty-eight minutes." He turned on his heel and disappeared back into the hauler.

"Back to work, everyone," Delroy snapped, dropping his prima-donna pose. "Let's wrap this up. Kelsey, are you ready? Tuck your helmet under your arm and look like you're walking into the teeth of the storm, okay. Battling the elements. Racing against the wind."

"Yeah, Kelsey, get out there and take one for the team," one of her over-the-wall pit crew said, grinning evilly.

"I'll pretend I'm walking into Victory Lane instead." She waved him off with a laugh and a shrug. Being the only girl in a family of four boys had prepared her well for dealing with her all-male teammates. Their teasing was good-natured and she didn't take offense. PDQ Racing was one of the smaller teams in NASCAR. This spread in

American Sports was an opportunity not to be missed. They all knew that as well as she did and were there for support as much as to tease the life out of her.

"Ready." She moistened her lips, splayed her fingers on her hips and braced herself for the blast of the big fan as she caught a glimpse of Delroy's assistant lifting his hand to flip the switch. A moment later, the fan roared to life propelling a choking cloud of dust and grit—straight into her eyes.

"WELL, MATT, WHAT DO YOU think of the setup here?"

"Not bad," Dr. Matt Abrams conceded as he followed his old friend and college roommate, Jamie Eagleson, into the tiny, closet-size space set aside for the doctors presiding over the infield care center during events at the track.

"We can treat half a dozen patients here at once, take care of anything from a sprained ankle to a major coronary incident and everything in between, and all you can say is 'not bad'?" Jamie was a big bear of a man with shaggy hair, a beard and gifted hands. A neurosurgeon and trauma specialist, he also had contracts with a number of racetracks across the southeast to manage their infield care centers. "Hell, I could operate here if I had to."

"Let's hope it doesn't come to that," Matt said, shaking his head. "The woman who went into labor last year at Darlington was excitement enough for me." Matt was an orthopedic surgeon. Delivering babies was something he hadn't done since medical school. Jamie, however, thrived on that kind of excitement.

"Piece of cake. Now if it had been twins…" Spending his weekends at the racetrack, tending to injuries—some of them serious and occasionally life-threatening—and ailments of fans and employees, drivers and team members was what Jamie did for relaxation. "You've got to admit being here in the middle of all the action beats sitting at home in Charlotte waiting for Monday morning to roll around again." He looked through the doorway into the main room of the care center, locked his hands behind his head and leaned back in his chair with a satisfied look on his face. "This is the life."

Matt wasn't so sure he agreed with that particular senti- ment, but his friend was right about one thing. Being here did beat sitting around in his Charlotte condo feeling sorry for himself, which is what Jamie declared he'd been doing for the better part of the past six months. He'd had good reason to have gone to ground, though. He figured it took at least that long to get over a broken relationship and a broken heart—and to mourn the loss of a baby.

The radio on the counter of the treatment area crackled to life. "EMT Unit 16 to Infield Base."

"Go ahead," one of the two registered nurses on duty re- sponded. Both of the nurses were male this race cycle, both veterans and former combat medics. Matt had no qualms about their qualifications or those of the EMTs working out on the track.

"We've got a seven-year-old boy here who shut his foot in the door of his parents' RV. He's got three badly lacer- ated toes. Our ETA's five minutes to your door."

"Time to go to work," Jamie said, "Want to assist?"

"No, I think I'll watch," Matt responded. A little boy. The emotions stirred by the memory of his wife's miscar- riage were too close to the surface right now.

Jamie gave him a hard stare that told him he knew what he was thinking. "Sure thing, buddy. There'll be something for you before too much longer. The campers will be pulling in all day long."

"Great. Sniffles and fever and upset stomachs, diarrhea and sunstroke. Sounds like a weekend to remember."

"Ain't it grand." Jamie grinned and looked as if he meant it.

Jamie was right about "something" coming along, but it wasn't a camper who'd eaten one deep-fried turkey leg too many. Not ten minutes after the sobbing little boy was carried into one of the treatment bays and Jamie had gone to work cleaning and suturing the mangled toes, all the while talking and soothing both his patient and the distraught parents, the radio crackled to life again.

"Female patient with a foreign object in her left eye."

Jamie looked up from his task. "Looks like you're up, bro."

Before Matt could think of an excuse to let one of the RNs handle the case, the door opened and half a dozen figures spilled into the care center, with a medium-height, medium-size woman in a green-and-blue team uniform and PDQ Racing cap at their center. A sterile bandage was taped over her left eye. She was talking soothingly to a distressed little man dressed all in black with at least three cameras dangling from straps around his neck. "It's all right, Delroy. It's just a cinder in my eye. I'll be fine. I'll get it checked out and we can go back and finish the shoot."

"But how?" the photographer, if that's what he was, moaned. "Your eye's red as fire."

"I'll wear my sunglasses. Every NASCAR driver gets photographed with sunglasses. It'll work, you'll see," she said, but Matt detected an undercurrent of anxiety in her low, honey-mellow voice, even if no one else picked up on it.

"Get these people out of my surgery," Jamie growled

from across the room as his nurse swept the curtain closed around the bed where he was working.

The sound of his friend's voice released Matt from the strange paralysis that had gripped him since the door had opened and the woman had entered the room. "You heard the man," he said to the second RN.

The lead EMT stayed put to give his report. The woman's team members who knew the drill were already moving toward the waiting room area. The media types, including the little man in black with the cameras, were no match for a former combat Navy medic, no matter how much they fussed and fumed. Thirty seconds later, Matt was alone and face-to-face with his patient.

"Hi," she said. "I'm Kelsey Kendall."

She smiled and it curved her mouth and spread upward to her eyes. Well, eye, he supposed, was the most accurate term since he could only see one. But what an eye—sea-green and flecked with gold and honey, surrounded by lush sable lashes. The wattage of that smile could have powered the track lighting for a night race. "And you are?" she asked, laying aside her ball cap. Hair the color of an antique gold coin spilled out from under the cap and over her shoulders.

"Matt Abrams," he said, his gaze momentarily snagged by the silken fall.

She nodded a polite response and then looked past him. "Is someone crying?" she asked as the little boy's hiccuping sobs came faintly from across the room. "A little one?" She seemed to have forgotten her own injury as she cocked her head toward the sound.

"Seven-year-old," Matt assured her. "Lacerated toes. My partner's fixing him up."

"He's going to be okay, right?'

"Sure."

"Good. I hate to hear little kids cry. I helped raise two younger brothers. It's big-sister conditioning."

Just then, the curtain around Jamie's cubicle swept open and the little kid sitting on the table leaned forward to look across the small space that separated the beds. "What happened to you?" he sniffed, rubbing his hand across his eyes as Jamie finished bandaging his injured foot.

"I got a cinder in my eye," Kelsey said, smiling. "What happened to you?"

"I shut my foot in the door," the kid said, looking as if he might start howling again. "I almost cut my toes off."

"Yikes. I'm glad that didn't happen."

"I have five stitches," the boy boasted, his sobs winding down to an occasional hiccup.

"You're really brave." Kelsey was sincere, not condescending as most adults would sound.

"I guess I am."

"Time to go back to the camper, big fella'" the child's father said, scooping him into his arms. "Let the doc look at the lady's eye."

The little boy wasn't done with his patient yet. "You're wearing a uniform. Are you on a team?"

"I am. I drive the No. 432 car for PDQ Racing," Kelsey said patiently, although Matt suspected she must be in a fair amount of discomfort.

"Wow! A lady driver. Like Shelley Green?"

"I hope to be that good someday."

"Can I have your autograph?"

"Jared, the lady's hurt," the boy's mother scolded. "She doesn't have time to sign an autograph for you."

"I only have a cinder in my eye," Kelsey assured her. Without missing a beat she picked up her discarded cap. She leaned forward and handed the cap to the child. "There. That's for being so brave."

A small grubby hand closed around the cap. "Thanks."

"Hang on to it, son. Someday this lady might be a champion."

Kelsey grinned. "Not *might be*. I intend to be one."

Matt swept the curtain shut as Kelsey waved goodbye. "Cute kid," Kelsey said, turning her attention to him.

"Yeah. Cute kid." He was a cute kid. Matt felt a familiar, sharp sting in the region of his heart. He refocused the subject to the business at hand so he wouldn't be able to dwell on his loss. "Want to tell me what happened to your eye?"

"I was striding into the 'heart of the storm.' They were using this big fan to blow my hair around and I ended up with a cinder in my eye." Kelsey smiled again. Matt had thought her first smile was high-voltage, but this one was incandescent, a little crooked on one side, spontaneous and unstudied, and it just about took his breath away. Maybe Jamie was right. Maybe he had been sitting alone in his condo too much if he was going to react this forcefully to a stranger's smile.

"I beg your pardon?"

She lifted her hand and gave a little wave toward the waiting room. "We're doing a shoot for *American Sports*. The magazine," she continued when Matt failed to respond. "You've heard of it, haven't you?"

"I've seen the bathing-suit issue." He'd said the wrong thing. She stiffened and the friendly smile disappeared.

"This isn't for the bathing-suit issue," she said. Her voice had turned to ice.

"Okay, we're straight on that. No bathing suits. It's probably a good thing. I imagine if you'd been wearing a bikini you'd have more than a cinder in your eye to worry about." Good Lord, what in the world had he let himself say that for? How unprofessional could he get?

She was silent for a moment or two, as if she was deciding whether to be offended by his comeback. "You're probably right," she said after another short silence and smiled.

Matt smiled back. He couldn't help himself. This smile, like the others, transformed her face, took her from merely pretty to, well, not beautiful—her features were too strong and clear-cut to be termed beautiful—but *unique* and *appealing* were certainly adjectives that could be applied to Kelsey Kendall.

"Let's have a look at that eye," he said and received his second shock of the day when he looked down and found his hands were trembling.

CHAPTER TWO

KELSEY WASN'T USED TO lying awake in her bed at 4:00 a.m. the day before a race. But here she was tossing and turning—and aching all over. At least her neck and shoulders were aching, worse than she could remember. She'd been trying to ignore the pain but she couldn't. What if there was something really wrong with her? Something major? She really ought to go to the doctor. Have some tests. Put an end to the awful thoughts squirreling around in her brain.

What if she had a brain tumor?

Or some kind of disabling muscular disease?

Or arthritis, like her dad's aunt, that would be so devastating she wound up in a wheelchair instead of behind the wheel of her race car?

No way. She wasn't giving up her ride in NASCAR for any reason—at least not until she won a championship.

She got up and padded into the bathroom of her motor home. It was an older model but well maintained, and best of all, it was paid for with her winnings in open-wheel cars over the past five seasons. She'd won seven races and come in second at Indianapolis the year before. Jim Latimer had seen that race and offered her a ride in NASCAR shortly after. She'd jumped at the chance. Who wouldn't? And she intended to stay strapped into her seat until she won a championship. No more second-place finishes for her.

She flicked on the light above the sink to search for the bottle of anti-inflammatory pills she always kept there. They were the kind you could buy in any drugstore, nothing that needed a prescription. She took as few as possible. She didn't want anyone to know about the pain—not her team owner, not her sponsor, not her family. But she couldn't go on hurting like this, waking up in the middle of the night tossing and turning and scaring herself silly.

The doctor who had removed the tiny speck of dust from her eye the other day at the infield care center—what was his name? Arps? Abraham? Abrams? That was it. Matt Abrams—maybe she could ask him what to do? Strictly hypothetically, of course. She was supposed to see him this morning anyway so that he could certify she was fit to race. She studied her eye in the mirror. No swelling, no redness, no more pain. That was good. Visual acuity was way too important in her sport to take any chances with an injury to her eye, no matter how minor a scratch it was.

She downed two of the tablets with a grimace and crawled back into bed. She'd just steer the conversation into those hypothetical questions about an aching neck and shoulders and see what Dr. Abrams had to say. Men were easy enough to manipulate that way—most of them, anyway, she amended, eliminating her team owner and her crew chief from that description.

She lay down in her queen-size bed that took up ninety percent of the space in the bedroom and closed her eyes, finding an image of the brown-haired, brown-eyed surgeon superimposed behind her eyelids. Maybe she should add him to that short list, she decided, picturing his squared-off jaw and unsmiling mouth. Dr. Matt Abrams hadn't seemed all that interested in conversation of any kind while he treated her, but her intuition told her he was a man who could be trusted. Professionally, at least. She couldn't assume anything about him personally. She'd never seen him before yesterday and didn't know him at all.

But she'd like to.

She shied away from the provocative thought. Driving was all she had time to think about these days. Not relationships. Not handsome, cranky surgeons with strong, surprisingly gentle hands.

Enough!

She turned onto her back, wincing as she tried to get comfortable against the half-dozen pillows she kept piled up around her. No more thinking about Dr. Matt Abrams as a man. What she needed was a healer. She just hoped this morning he'd be in a better mood because she was talking a good game to herself now, but deep down inside she was scared to death of what she might learn.

"LET ME GET THIS straight," Matt said, motioning Kelsey to take a seat on the exam table. She hopped up on the high gurney with the grace of a natural-born athlete, a dancer, maybe, strong and graceful. Jamie and the two RNs were catching up on paperwork in the office and for the moment, at least, there weren't any other emergencies to be taken care of, so he had a free moment or two to study his patient and come up with fanciful observations like that one. "You say you have this friend—a guy on your team—who's having a lot of neck and shoulder pain?"

She was wearing her driver's uniform again today, and while it fit her rounded curves very well indeed, he was beginning to wonder what she'd look like in civilian clothes—a slinky little black dress, maybe, and high heels. Jeez. This was an even more unprofessional lapse than the first one.

"His hands and wrists, too. It's like they're always going to sleep," Kelsey responded, not looking directly at him but at a point just past his left shoulder.

He put the image of her in the black dress firmly out of his mind and began to pay attention to the flesh-and-blood woman in front of him. He'd only met her once before, but he was almost positive she was lying to him about the "guy on her team," but he pretended not to notice. "It could be a lot of things. Arthritis, a bone spur, even something more serious than that," he said, not really quite focused on the question as he began his examination. He was still trying to absorb the voltage of looking directly into those sea-green eyes of hers and it took a lot of concentration.

"Like a brain tumor or something?" she said, her voice turning a little hard around the edges, as though she were working to keep any emotion from seeping into it.

"Brain tumor? It's a possibility," he conceded. "Not very likely, though. And not my field of expertise." He switched off the lighted scope he'd used for his examination. "Your eye looks fine," he continued, keeping to the matter at hand. "Is it giving you any discomfort?" She shook her head no. "Good. Just what I wanted to hear." The tiny scratch on her cornea had almost healed overnight as he'd expected it would. He'd have her continue the medicated drops he'd given her for a few more days, though, to be on the safe side. You didn't want to take any chances with an eye injury, no matter how minor—especially for a NASCAR driver.

"Great," she said, then returned to her original subject. "Now about my teammate. Could it really be a brain tumor?"

She was one stubborn and single-minded lady.

Like Lisa? A woman so dedicated to her profession she had jeopardized her pregnancy to pursue her career.

"Like I said, highly unlikely," he responded gruffly.

"I'm glad to hear that." She smiled, obviously relieved, and he smiled back. He couldn't help himself—just like yesterday—and the comparison to his ex-fiancée didn't seem as apt as it had a moment before. Stock-car racing was a physically demanding sport, even more so for a woman. He began to suspect she was talking about herself and not a teammate. "The symptoms you mentioned could be caused by a number of conditions—hypothetically speaking."

"Like what?"

He opened his mouth to name the most likely culprits when the radio on the counter came to life. "Wreck in Turn Two. Units 103 and 104 on the move."

The go-or-go-home cars were qualifying for the Sunday race. He didn't know who was out on the track at that particular moment but she did. "That's Barry Webster's car. I didn't hear anything. Hope it's not serious." She slipped the sunglasses she'd been twirling between her fingers onto the top of her head, shifting her long, fine blond hair. He watched as it resettled itself over her shoulders and found he had to take a breath to relieve the tightness in his chest. She looked around her with the slightly trapped expression that most drivers wore when they entered the building. NASCAR drivers didn't much like being in the care center for any reason, and he couldn't say he blamed them.

"I'd better be going," she said, slipping down off the table and turning toward the back entrance as Jamie and the RNs came hustling out of the office. "Now, about my friend… What do you suggest?"

"If you like, I could run some tests."

She swiveled her head, alarm darkening her gorgeous eyes. "I…I wasn't talking about myself," she assured him hastily.

"Are you sure?" he asked, wondering why he was pressing the matter. He preferred to attribute his persistence to his concern for her health and not to wanting to see her again somewhere outside this cinder-block building—even if it was in his office at the clinic in Charlotte.

She made eye contact with him this time, and the shock of it surged through him like an adrenaline rush. "Okay," she said. "It's me." She looked down at her hands, flexed her long fingers, hands and fingers that seemed too delicate to wrestle almost two tons of stock car around a track at speeds reaching somewhere in the vicinity of 180 miles an hour. When she looked up again he saw the ocean in winter, sea-green darkened with worry and concern. "What time do you want me there?"

CHAPTER THREE

"MATT, THERE'S A CALL for you on Line Three."

He turned away from the dreary view of the clinic parking lot outside his office window to confront his nurse, who was also his mother's twin sister, his aunt Darla. "It's Kelsey Kendall." She raised her eyebrows a fraction of an inch. *"The Kelsey Kendall?"* She had been with him since his first day in practice and ruled his office with an iron fist in a velvet glove. She was also an avid racing fan, and he knew she was curious about the battery of tests he'd ordered for one of her favorite drivers, but she had refrained from asking.

"Yes," he said, glancing at his watch. "She was my six o'clock appointment." His stomach growled hungrily. "She's late," he frowned as he picked up the phone.

"Dr. Abrams, hi. It's Kelsey Kendall. I'm calling to apologize for being late for our appointment. I've hit a snag," she said, exasperation evident in her honey-rich tones.

"Stuck in traffic?" he asked, striving to keep the impatience out of his voice. It had been a long day. He'd been in the O.R. before 7:00 a.m. He'd done rounds and seen patients. He was tired and hungry and he wanted to call it a day. But he also wanted to see Kelsey again.

"Not exactly," she replied. "More like stuck in your parking lot."

"What?" he turned his back on his eavesdropping aunt and looked out the window again. It was a gray overcast day with rain threatening before nightfall. There were a dozen or so cars in the parking lot, most he recognized as belonging to other doctors and their staff. One was a good-looking sports car, black and low-slung, the kind a sexy female race-car driver might own. Sexy female? He never, ever, allowed himself to consider a patient in those terms. He'd better get hold of himself. "Are you having car problems?" he asked, adding a layer of professional reserve to his voice.

"No, I'm having paparazzi problems. There are a couple of racing news reporters and a particularly nosy blogger hanging around out here. Someone must have gotten the word out that I was at the hospital having those tests yesterday. I really don't want to talk to them. I hope you understand." Her voice was still light and steady, but as that day in the infield care center at Bristol he could sense the underlying anxiety.

"Do you want to reschedule?" Now that he was looking for them he spotted an SUV with a couple of guys in it. The reporters, maybe? A VW Bug with a woman in a peasant skirt and long blouse leaning against it, what appeared to be a small video camera in her left hand. The blogger?

Good Lord, Kelsey was right; she was being followed.

Of course, she was an easy target to spot if that was her in that six-figure car. He squinted and made out a female figure behind the wheel. Her features were shadowed by a wide-billed ball cap but something about the tilt of her head, the angle of her chin, was familiar. Kelsey. "Couldn't we discuss my tests over the phone?" she asked hopefully.

"We could," he said, surprised to find he would be disappointed if he didn't see her in person. "But I'd rather not."

His aunt had been listening unashamedly from the doorway. He frowned at her but she ignored it. Smiling, she crossed her arms across her chest and stayed put.

"I could buy you a burger," Kelsey said. "I don't know about you but I'm starved, and I know a great diner in Mooresville where we won't be disturbed."

The woman in the peasant skirt was scanning the parking lot with her video camera. From where he was standing, it looked as if she was zooming in on Kelsey. Jeez, is that how it worked when you were famous? You couldn't even visit your doctor without someone wanting to film it and spread the word across cyberspace and around the world?

No one deserved that kind of treatment, no matter what they did for a living. It would be an unusual consultation, but he decided to say yes. He wanted to see Kelsey again, and not just because she was a patient he had sworn to counsel and heal. She was one very intriguing lady. He picked up the heavy manila envelope that contained her MRI and X-ray results and tapped it against the desk. "All right," he said. "I'll meet you for dinner. How do I get to this place?"

MAUDIE'S DOWN HOME DINER was an institution with the people in the NASCAR world. Tucked away on a side street in Mooresville, it was convenient to most of the race-team shops. It was frequented by local residents as well as team members and drivers and even an occasional owner or two, but very few outsiders found their way into Maudie's. It was one place Kelsey knew she would have at least a modicum of privacy for her meeting with Dr. Abrams—privacy from her fans and the media, at least, if not the rest of NASCAR. Looking around, she counted half a dozen drivers and crew chiefs, her teammate Bart Branch and his twin brother among them.

And best of all, the food was delicious.

She figured Dr. Matt Abrams could use a home-cooked meal—he had that look about him—and Maudie's was the place to buy it for him. Kelsey knew her way around a racing V-8 as well as most shop mechanics, but beyond nuking a frozen dinner or reheating takeout, a kitchen was as foreign to her as the surface of the moon.

Kelsey waved a greeting to Sheila Trueblood, the new owner of Maudie's who was behind the counter herself on this fairly quiet Wednesday. She settled into one of the red vinyl-upholstered booths with a view of the street and the door. If it were a Tuesday, Kelsey would be in the back room along with the other Tuesday Tarts, a fellowship of NASCAR women spanning three generations. But tonight she was alone.

Kelsey figured she was at least ten minutes ahead of Matt Abrams, even though she'd had to take a roundabout way back to Mooresville to shake off the persistent reporters who'd spotted her leaving the clinic parking lot. The men in the SUV had required a little evasive maneuvering, but the blogger in her underpowered Bug had never been in the race. She smiled to herself and settled down to wait.

Sheila, about the same age as Kelsey, came out from behind the counter and approached the booth. "Hi, Kelsey," Sheila said. "Sorry about your finish at Bristol. Sure was bad luck, you losing your engine that way."

"That's racin'. That's Bristol." Kelsey shrugged and smiled, hoping the grin hid her chagrin at her less-than-stellar performance at the famed short track. She'd made a rookie mistake, missed a gear and killed her engine.

Moving from open-wheel cars to stock cars was tough enough, but short tracks seemed to be her downfall. Martinsville, next up in the series, was as idiosyncratic a track as Bristol. She already had butterflies just thinking about driving it.

"You'll be back up on the wheel next week. You'll do fine," Sheila predicted in her usual confident way. Everything about the diner's owner was quick, Kelsey thought. She was lean, fast-moving, tough as nails and a good friend when you needed one.

"I'll do my best."

A young, doe-eyed, dark-haired waitress approached the table. "Kelsey, this is Mellie Donovan," Sheila said. "She's working here now."

"It's nice to meet you." Mellie's smile never quite reached her big, sad eyes.

"Nice to meet you, too, Mellie," Kelsey returned, accepting the menu Mellie offered. "A…friend…is joining me in a few minutes so I'll need another one of these."

"Coming right up. Can I get you something to drink?"

"A glass of sweet tea."

"I'll be back with both those things just as soon as I check on the guys at the counter."

"That would be the Branch brothers," Sheila said in an undertone. "Bart's practically a fixture since I hired Mellie."

"Bart has always had an eye for a pretty girl."

"She's got the makings of a good waitress. Lord knows, I need one."

"Is she from around here?" Kelsey asked. Mooresville was a small town, the kind where everybody knew everybody else, but Mellie hadn't looked familiar. It appeared as if it would be longer than a minute or two before Mellie came back to the table. Bart Branch seemed intent on keeping her right where she was at the moment—talking to him.

"She's from out west, somewhere. She's all alone in the world, poor kid. She's trying to raise a baby sister since their mama died, and her not much more than a baby herself."

"That takes some spine," Kelsey said, thankful as always that she had her brothers and parents to fall back on when she needed support.

"Sure does. Wow! Is that the friend you've been waiting for?" Sheila asked, her eyes widening in appreciation as she watched the front door of the diner swing open to admit Matt Abrams.

"That's him."

He was wearing a black leather jacket over a light blue dress shirt, open at the neck, and charcoal-gray slacks. No long white doctor's coat to give his profession away.

"Kelsey, girl, you've been holding out on us," Sheila said with a grin. "What a specimen. Where did you find him?"

"I met him at Bristol," Kelsey said. Better to stick to the truth as much as possible. She held up a hand to attract Matt's attention. He waved back and began threading his way through the busy diner. "And it's not what you're thinking, Sheila," she said under her breath. "I barely know the man."

"Well, if I were you I'd use this evening to get to know him better. A lot better. Hello," Sheila said, giving Matt a megawatt smile. "Welcome to Maudie's."

"Thank you," he said, coming to a halt beside the booth. He was carrying a big manila envelope. Her test results. Kelsey's heart rate increased for the second time. The first uptick had happened when she'd glimpsed Matt walking through the door.

"Have a seat," Kelsey said. She couldn't focus on anything but the envelope he carried. The ache in her neck and shoulders began to intensify. Her fingers tingled and she laced her hands together to stop them from trembling. Her future was inside that envelope, and the man who carried it had come to pass judgment on her life-long dream of winning a NASCAR Sprint Cup Series championship.

"DID YOU HAVE TROUBLE finding the place?" Kelsey asked him after the timid-looking young waitress had taken his drink order and topped off Kelsey's tea.

"No problem. Your directions were right on the money." Matt looked around the diner, all red vinyl upholstery, chrome trim and black-and-white tile on the floor. Not just retro-style, he suspected, but the real thing. "I've lived around the Concord/Mooresville area my whole life and never knew this place was here."

"That's what we like about it," she said with that cover-girl smile of hers. He felt his pulse accelerate a dozen beats a minute, even though he'd steeled himself not to react to her as anything more than a patient.

"Did you have any trouble losing your posse?" he asked gruffly.

She tilted her head and gave him a look. "No," she said.

"I didn't think you would. But it must be damned hard to keep a low profile in a car like that one."

Lord, could he sound any more priggish if he tried?

She shrugged off his jab. "The dealership is one of my associate sponsors. I'm contractually obligated to be seen in that sexy little number."

"Makes it hard to stay inconspicuous, doesn't it?"

"There is that. She's a sweet ride, though."

The waitress returned, set his drink in front of him and

waited, order pad in hand. "The special's a meat-loaf sandwich with mashed potatoes on the side."

"Sheila makes the best meat loaf in the world," Kelsey said. "That's what I'm having."

He closed his menu. "Sounds good to me." It did, too. He hadn't had a home-cooked meal in a long time. Lisa hadn't had the time or inclination to cook, and while he knew his way around a kitchen, cooking for himself always seemed a waste of time.

"Two specials." Kelsey waited until the waitress walked away. "Thanks for coming, Doc," she said when they were alone. "I'm sorry to have inconvenienced you this way."

He waved off her apology. "No problem. Do you want to discuss your tests now or wait until after we've eaten?"

She took a deep breath as though he had asked her if she was ready to jump off a cliff blindfolded. "Now," she said, clearing her throat.

He laid his hand on the envelope. "Normally I'd show you the films but I figure you don't want to draw that much attention, correct?"

"Yes."

He nodded. "Okay, here's what I see. The MRI shows the beginning of degenerative disc disease."

The color faded from her cheeks, leaving her face pale and accentuating a scattering of freckles across the bridge of her nose he hadn't noticed before. "My grandmother suffered from something like that. She spent the last three years of her life in a wheelchair."

"I'm sorry to hear that," he said, and he was. "The tendency to the condition is hereditary in some cases."

"And I already have the symptoms. Grandma was sixty-five before she started having problems. I'm only twenty-six."

"You lead a very active and physically demanding life. That can contribute to the acceleration of the condition—" He never got to finish what he'd been going to say.

"You're saying I have to give up my ride in NASCAR, aren't you?"

He hadn't intended to say that, not in so many words, but he was going to advise her to consider it. Cervical degenerative disc disease could become a very serious and debilitating condition if left untreated. He opened his mouth to refute the accusation but she didn't give him a chance. She jumped up from her chair. "I have to go."

"Kelsey, wait." He stood, too.

"I'm not giving up my ride. I worked too hard to make it to the Show. I won't do it." She backed away from the table. She was clearly distressed but she kept her voice low so they wouldn't be overheard.

"You aren't listening." He held out his hand to slow her down, to give him a chance to finish what he'd been going to say.

"I heard you loud and clear. All I've ever wanted is to win a NASCAR championship. I'm not going to stop racing until I do." She hurried toward the exit, leaving the waitress standing with two meat-loaf specials in her hands, staring openmouthed.

"Is she leaving?" Mellie asked.

"I guess so," Matt said grinding his back teeth. What had gotten into Kelsey? She had panicked over a discussion of a condition that might or might not become more serious a long time in the future.

A cold wave coursed across his nerve endings. Maybe it hadn't been the memory of her grandmother's suffering that had upset her. It had been contemplating even the possibility of giving up her racing career that had set her off. Just like Lisa, he thought with a sharp, angry pain around his heart. She was just like Lisa, willing to risk everything to pursue her dreams.

He had thought—hoped, at least—that she was different than Lisa, but she wasn't. Let that be a lesson to him. He picked up the manila envelope and turned to leave.

·"Is Kelsey coming back?" the bewildered waitress asked. She looked down at the heaped plates of food in her hands. "Are you leaving?"

He'd forgotten about the waitress and the meat-loaf specials. His stomach was tied up in knots. He wasn't interested in food, only in finding Kelsey Kendall and giving her a piece of his mind. But he had no intention of creating a bigger scene than they'd already had. Heads were turning at nearby tables. As angry as he was at her, he also couldn't help feeling protective of his erstwhile patient.

"Something came up. Kelsey had to leave," he explained, working hard to keep his tone normal and even. He dug in his back pocket for his billfold. "How much do I owe you?" He pulled out a couple of bills. "Keep the change."

"Thanks," she said. "Shall I box these up for you?"

"Sure," he said. "Why not?" Kelsey was long gone. He'd never catch her in her sleek black car. He didn't even want to. If she wanted any more medical advice from him, she could call his office to make an appointment.

And apologize.

Then, and only then, would they talk.

CHAPTER FOUR

SHE WASN'T SURE HOW she was going to go about this apology thing. She'd picked up her phone a dozen times over the past five days to call Matt's office and do just that, but each time she'd never connected. Either she couldn't get a signal from where she was in the garage or on the track, or she had been interrupted by teammates or sponsor commitments.

Or, let's be honest about it, she thought ruefully, *you really just chickened out.*

Well, she didn't need a cell-phone signal now. She was standing less than twenty feet from the infield care center at Martinsville, the iconic, paper-clip-shaped short track that was as big a challenge to her as Bristol had been the week before. She'd learned through the garage grapevine that Matt Abrams was here, too, serving as one of the infield care-center doctors again this race weekend.

All she had to do was press the admittance buzzer and in less than a minute they would be face-to-face again.

Maybe that was why she was sleeping so badly, why her neck and shoulders were so stiff and sore—not because she had a debilitating disease that would eventually cripple her, but because she was so tense and anxious she couldn't relax.

for one of the drivers whose wife had a baby early this morning. The woman's got game," Jamie said approvingly, taking another bite of his hot dog. "She'll drive anything with four wheels and an engine."

Matt stared at the screen. Sure enough, there was Kelsey, dressed in a red-and-silver uniform emblazoned with the name of an area grocery chain, probably a onetime sponsor for the local race. She was standing beside a car with the same red-and-silver color scheme and lettering as her uniform. She was talking earnestly with a female reporter with huge earphones on her head and a microphone in her hand. Kelsey looked relaxed, and she smiled as she spoke. He couldn't see her glorious sea-green eyes behind the mirrored sunglasses she wore, but Matt got the feeling that she wasn't really as relaxed as she appeared. He took a couple of steps closer to the screen. Was she in pain? He found himself studying her every movement, every change of expression to read her comfort level.

"You've got it bad, old man," Jamie said, pitching his wadded up wax-paper sandwich wrapper into the wastebasket.

"What?" Matt swiveled his head away from the TV screen.

"I said you've got it bad." Jamie angled his head toward the screen.

"Don't be ridiculous," Matt said. "She's a patient. She's my responsibility."

"Okay," Jamie responded with a grin. "But I've never seen you staring at any of your hip-replacement patients with your mouth hanging open that way."

"I have no personal interest in Kelsey Kendall," he said and knew he was lying the moment the words left his mouth.

"Sure, sure," Jamie scoffed.

"I do not have personal relationships with my patients," Matt declared, perhaps to remind himself as much as his friend.

Jamie wiped the grin from his face. They both took their profession too seriously to cross the line between doctor/patient relationships. "If you come to your senses and want to start one, I'll be more than happy to take over her case for you."

"What case?" Matt said, wishing he could take Jamie up on his offer but at the same time not wanting to release Kelsey from his care, however nominal it was at the moment. "She hasn't spoken a word to me since she walked out of the diner."

THEY WERE A HUNDRED LAPS into the race. She hadn't driven a NASCAR Nationwide Series car yet this season but the setup on Casey Hilliard's—the driver whose ride she'd taken for the afternoon so that he could be with his wife and newborn son—car was good and she was running in fifteenth position. Not a bad place to be with a strange car and a crew who were as unfamiliar to her as she was to them.

She was glad Jim Latimer and Dane had agreed to let her take the ride this afternoon. She'd never driven Martinsville before, and today's experience would be invaluable tomorrow when she was driving in the NASCAR Sprint Cup Series race. All she had to do now was keep out of trouble and she had a good chance of finishing in the top ten.

Not two laps later, her optimism proved misplaced.

A spurt of white smoke signaled an engine failure in one of the cars on the straightaway ahead of her. Her spotter saw it, too, and began shouting in her earphones. She wasn't used to taking directions from him—he was Hilliard's regular spotter, not hers—but she paid attention to what he said. The trail of smoke ballooned into a cloud as the cars on either side were drawn into the fray and visibility dropped to zero, all in less than a handful of seconds. Race cars began to scatter, hoping to avoid the wreck.

"Stay low! Stay low!" the spotter yelled into her headphones. Kelsey's instinct was to go high. She had seen three cars already heading for the inside apron. But the spotter was high atop the grandstand with a better view of the track ahead. She pulled the wheel to the left, fought the urge to stand on the brake and dived into the smoke, hoping to come out on the other side with her race car all in one piece.

She almost made it.

CHAPTER FIVE

"MATT, BE READY AT Station 2. We have four drivers involved in the wreck in Turn Three. First ambulance ETA is 90 seconds." Jamie was already at the scrub sink washing up. Matt dragged his eyes away from the TV monitor and followed him.

He wasn't sure, but he had the sinking feeling that Kelsey's car had been involved in the pileup. Four cars damaged; at least that many more able to drive behind the wall to the garage stalls under their own power; one or two others with minor damage that would be dealt with in the pits.

All the drivers had walked away from the melee, a testament to the safety standards NASCAR so vigorously enforced, but he hadn't been able to tell yet if Kelsey had been one of them. He watched the looping replay of the wreck from the corner of his eye as he washed up, and then gave a quick check to the emergency tray beside the exam bed where he would be working. The RNs on duty this week were regulars who worked every race at the track. Everything he needed was well within reach. All he had to do now was wait.

Then the wide door swung open, letting in bright spring sunshine, a cacophony of sound and bustling movement. A scowling driver and EMT entered first, followed by a second and third, all males. No Kelsey. Maybe he'd been mistaken that her car was involved. He strained to see beyond the figures filling the doorway but couldn't pick her out of the crowd.

He locked away his curiosity and unsettling anxiety about a woman he barely knew and concentrated on examining his patient, a very upset and angry young man who had been running well up at the front of the pack until he had been slammed into the wall by the first two cars involved.

Matt was new to this kind of medical duty but knew better than to try to make conversation with an upset driver. He examined his patient quickly but thoroughly, double-checked the numbers on his vital signs and turned him loose to meet first with his wife, who had been brought to the small private waiting room of the care center, and then with the media waiting outside.

"Hello, Doctor." The voice was honey, smooth and rich, with an undernote of pure heat. Matt spun on his heel and found himself staring directly into Kelsey's sea-green eyes. Jamie was dealing with the last of the drivers' paperwork. Two or three EMTs and emergency personnel were still milling around the treatment room; the younger of the two RNs was cleaning up the treatment bays, readying them for the next patient, whoever that might be. But at this moment, Matt felt as if he and the woman who occupied so much of his thoughts might as well have been alone in the world.

The older RN, the one who reminded him of his aunt, was standing by the curtain that could be pulled to isolate each exam bay. "Her vitals are steady and all within normal limits, Doctor." She handed him Kelsey's chart.

"Uh, thanks." He hoped he didn't look as off-center as he felt.

Kelsey had peeled off the jacket of her uniform. The fire-retardant undersuit every driver wore hugged her slim waist like a second skin. Matt felt his mouth go dry. "I hoped your car had made it through the wreck," he said, very much aware every word they spoke to each other could and would be overheard by half a dozen others.

"I almost did. Debris on the track cut down my right front tire. No one's fault, but I hit the safety barrier a pretty good lick. My car is toast," she finished with a frown that drew his attention to her arched brows and gold-tipped eyelashes.

"Any injuries to report?" he asked gruffly, picking up a scope to check for signs of a concussion or other head injury.

"No," she said, short and sharp. "Not a scratch."

"You're sure?" he prodded. "You weren't driving your own car. The seat in that one was built for a man who out-weighs you by fifty pounds or more." He wasn't a NASCAR engineer but he knew each seat was molded to the driver's individual body specifications to keep him from being knocked around in the cockpit during a race—or a wreck. Whatever modifications had been made to Kelsey's, it still wouldn't have been as formfitting as her own.

"I'm sure," she said. "Can I go now?"

"May I?" he asked, nodding toward her shoulder, ignoring her demand to be released. This wasn't Maudie's Diner. They were on his turf now.

She shrugged, knowing she had no other choice but to cooperate. He palpated her shoulder, feeling the firm delineation of bone and muscle. She was in good shape; probably worked out regularly. A woman would have to work hard to maintain that degree of upper-body strength. He probed a little harder and wasn't surprised when she winced at the pressure of his hand.

"It's just a bruise."

"I concur with your diagnosis."

She flushed. "Could we hurry this along? I want to get back to the garage."

"I thought you said the car was toast."

"I'm driving for a good team. We need the points. If they can get the car moving again, I can drive it," she insisted.

"I'm sure you can but I suggest you don't."

"What?"

"If you aggravate the injury any more today, you'll suffer for it tomorrow," he said bluntly.

"Are you refusing to release me to finish the race because I bruised my shoulder?" she asked incredulously. "That's ridiculous. Who's in charge here? I want to talk to whoever it is. Now!" She didn't raise her voice, as aware as he was of listening ears. She pulled her uniform jacket back on, jerking the heavy zipper up to her throat. She didn't wince, didn't frown at the movement, but he saw the slight narrowing of her eyes and knew the defiant gesture had caused her considerable pain.

"That won't be necessary. You're cleared to race again if you can get back on the track," he said as he grabbed the chart and slashed his signature across the release form. "I'm just giving you my professional opinion."

"When I want your opinion, I'll ask for it," she snapped, losing her temper and her cool for just a moment.

"I believe you already did."

She had the grace to look ashamed. "I have to go. My crew chief and the media will be waiting outside." She slid off the exam table and took the helmet the nurse handed her with a smile of thanks. The real one, the one that turned his insides to jelly.

"By the way," Matt said, for some reason determined to have the last word, "your eye has healed up just fine."

She gave him the cover-girl version of her smile, the one she bestowed on the world at large, and a wink. "I know it has," she said and sashayed out the door.

"Damn it," Matt said under his breath. She'd gotten away without apologizing again.

IT WAS A BEAUTIFUL early-spring night. The track was quiet, the garages and haulers locked until morning as per NASCAR regulations. Golf carts purred along the pathways as meetings broke up and team members headed to their hotel rooms and drivers retreated to the comfort of their motor homes, just as she would soon be doing.

Off in the distance, she heard music and laughter and smelled the sweet tang of wood smoke. All around the racetrack, Kelsey knew, were thousands and thousands of campers and motor homes in campgrounds and in the front yards and parking lots of surrounding homes and businesses, some only yards from the main gate. But at the moment, she felt as alone as she ever did at a NASCAR track.

She let her golf cart glide silently along a darkened access path until she was parked in the shadow of the infield care center. Matt Abrams would be coming off duty in a few minutes. She knew that because she had asked around; a casual question here and there to a team member who knew one of the track guards, who was dating the daughter of one of the EMT crew members, whose sister-in-law was one of the nurses who helped staff the facility. Unofficial, but highly effective, the NASCAR grapevine was almost as fast-moving as the cars themselves.

She owed the man an apology and she wasn't going

to be able to rest until she offered it. Her conscience was even more of an obstacle to a good night's sleep than the nagging ache in her neck and shoulders. She wished she'd been able to get it over with that afternoon, but that had been impossible. The grapevine had worked to her advantage this evening, but it would have been just as fast and efficient spreading word of any encounter between her and the good doctor.

She'd run out of excuses and delaying tactics. There was no one hanging around outside the care center but her. The door opened and a figure was silhouetted against the light from inside before it swung shut again. Tall, broad-shouldered, hair a little on the long side for her taste. It was him, all right, Doctor Perfect Male Specimen. Kelsey's heart tried to crawl up into her throat, but she swallowed hard and kept it where it belonged, banging away inside her chest.

Darn, but she needed to get herself under control. He was only a man, not all that different from her father or brothers. No, scratch that. He didn't remind her in the least of her father and her brothers, except perhaps in the way that she sensed, instinctively, that he was principled and honorable—beneath that standoffish, professional persona he wore like an impenetrable, invisible shell.

Another wave of reluctance washed over her. If she stayed where she was, didn't make a sound or a sudden movement to attract his attention, he would walk away into the night and she would be spared the embarrassment of an apology. But she wasn't going to do that. Those qualities she detected in him, the ones that drew her, were also qualities they shared. She had acted out of character the other evening at Maudie's. She had been flustered and upset, and she had behaved badly. She'd repeated the behavior again today. She couldn't—and wouldn't—be satisfied until she'd set things right.

She took a deep breath and said, "Hey, Doc, got a minute to spare?"

CHAPTER SIX

THERE IT WAS AGAIN, that sexy voice ringing in his ears. He ignored it. He'd gotten good at it over the past few days, except this time the voice wouldn't be denied.

"Over here," it said again. "Behind you."

Matt spun around. He could barely make out the shape of the golf cart sitting in the shadows of the care-center building. The figure in the driver's seat was even more indistinct, only vaguely feminine in shape and form. But there was no mistaking the gut-tightening sensuality of that come-hither voice.

"Hello, Kelsey," he said, proud of the fact that his voice didn't betray his inner turmoil. "You're out late."

"I've been waiting for you," she said candidly. The come-hither purr was gone, replaced with the soft, liquid vowels of a native North Carolinian. Somehow he found this unstudied tone of hers even more appealing.

"You have?" he asked, moving to stand beside her. "Why, may I ask?"

He sensed, rather than saw, her smile. Her tone was rueful. "You're not going to make this easy for me, are you?"

"Make what easy?"

"Do you mind getting inside the cart?" she asked. "I'd rather not be seen with you if we can avoid it."

"Ouch," he said.

"I didn't mean it that way," she said with a flare of temper. "You don't want to be on the receiving end of a media feeding frenzy, do you? That's what you'll get if rumors start flying about us being seen together."

"Okay. I get the point." He swung onto the empty seat beside her. His leg was mere inches from hers. He could feel the warmth of her body, smell the fragrance of her shampoo and the intoxicating scent of her skin. Warning alarms went off in his brain but he ignored them. "What is it you want to talk to me about?"

He could see her chest rise as she took a deep breath. "I want to apologize." She was wearing something white and gauzy, long-sleeved and open at the throat. It wasn't the first time he'd seen her out of uniform, but it was the first time he'd allowed himself to contemplate the soft feminine curves beneath the filmy top. "I hate having to do it for any reason, but especially when it's because I made a fool of myself."

"Um, which occasion are you referring to?"

She'd come to apologize and she wasn't finding it easy. He realized he didn't want to make it easy for her because if he did, she would say her piece and be gone in a matter of moments.

He wanted her to stay.

Her eyebrows pulled together in a quick frown. "I don't need the sarcasm," she said, but he got the impression she was trying to hide a grin.

"Sorry," he said, spreading both hands. "Please continue. I won't interrupt again." He not only wanted her to stay, he wanted her to be alone with him someplace dark and private. He hadn't even thought about a woman that way for six long months. Why now? Why Kelsey, who had many of the same qualities that had driven him and Lisa apart?

"Thank you," she said as formally as he had.

"It was a joke," he said. He hadn't used to be that way, so stuffed-shirt someone couldn't tell when he was making a joke.

She slanted him a look from the corner of her eye. "I know," she informed him. "You're not very good at it, though. Try smiling now and then. That might help."

"I'll do my best."

She took another breath. Here it comes, he thought. She would say she was sorry for having taken off like a bat out of hell Monday night. He would say, "No problem. Forget it," and that would be that. He would get out of the cart and she would drive off into the night—alone. Instead she surprised him again.

"Where are you staying?" she asked.

"I'm bunking in with a friend in a motor home just outside the gates. We're parked in someone's front yard."

She laughed, a spark of quicksilver in the darkness. "That's the way it's done at Martinsville. I can't invite you to my motor home, either. My youngest brother and a couple of his college buddies are camped out with me this weekend."

"That big sister thing again?"

"Yeah, I can't stop mothering him." She laughed, and he wanted to laugh with her. But he was out of practice, and the moment passed. "He's a good kid. He's going into the Marines this summer after he graduates." He heard the pride and the underlying anxiety in her voice that he bet she didn't know was there. "So I guess we do this right here." No more teasing, no more banter—her tone was

suddenly dead serious. He saw her hands clench and un-
clench on the steering wheel. He felt ashamed of his earlier
desire to make her work for his forgiveness.

"Kelsey, this isn't necessary." He wanted to reach out
and cover her hand with his own, stroke his fingers across
the soft skin of her wrist and inner arm, soothe away the
tension he could feel radiating from her.

"No, I need to do this," she said. "I want to apologize
for my behavior at Maudie's the other evening. There was
no excuse for running away like that. Not to mention leaving you stuck with the bill."

"The meat loaf was great," he said.

She refused to be led off topic. "Regardless. It was
childish and immature behavior. And while I'm at it I want
to apologize for what I said this afternoon, as well. You
were just doing your job."

"All right, I'll accept your apologies if you'll accept mine."

She half turned toward him. Their thighs brushed momentarily, and her arm was so close that if he shifted his
weight a fraction of an inch they would touch. "Why
should you apologize?"

"I should never have agreed to meet you at a public
place like Maudie's to talk about your medical condition
in the first place."

"And this afternoon?"

"You'd just been involved in a high-speed collision and
I picked a fight with you."

"I was in no way incapacitated," she reminded him. "I
could hold my own in an…exchange of opinions."

"You were shook up and I didn't help the situation insisting you stand down from your ride because of a
bruised shoulder."

She shrugged off his words. "You were doing your job. I was doing mine."

Kelsey was a woman completely focused on her career, no matter how detrimental it might be to her future health and well-being. The simple statement sent a jolt of warning through his nervous system. He needed to back off and fast, except he seemed unable to make himself stand up and walk away.

"I…I do want to discuss my…condition…with you someday soon," she said, looking straight ahead once more. It was back, that oddly vulnerable note in her voice that was so at odds with her diamond-hard public persona, "At an appropriate time and place, of course."

This wasn't the appropriate time or place for a medical consultation. But it was the perfect time, if not the perfect place, to kiss a beautiful woman. He reached out and touched her cheek with the tip of his finger before he could think better of it. "Kelsey," he said, meaning only to reassure her, to tell her not to worry about what might or might not happen many years down the road.

She turned her head, and starlight glistened in her eyes, teardrops she wouldn't let fall. In a heartbeat hot blood pooled low in his stomach and his body reacted with a predictable and age-old response. He ran his hand over the silkiness of the honey-gold spill of her hair, bent forward to place his mouth on hers. She didn't take her hands from the steering wheel; her mouth opened beneath his, and heat exploded inside him in a way he'd never experienced before.

"Kelsey?" He wasn't sure what he meant to say, but it didn't matter. He'd lost the ability to form any word but her name.

"Shh, just kiss me," she said. He made a sound of protest

against her lips. "We'll sort this all out later." She cupped her hands on either side of his face as though to keep him there, keep his mouth on hers. He stopped thinking altogether, stopped trying to analyze the chemical reaction that welded them together, and just let himself feel. He reached out and pulled her into his arms, and she came willingly, pliant against him. Her hands threaded into his hair, and she kissed him back with the same passion she gave to her racing.

He tightened his grip, wanting, needing, to have her as close as humanly possible. She tensed and a small moan escaped her lips, not one of passion, but of pain. Her shoulder. He'd completely forgotten the contusion she'd suffered earlier in the day. He dragged his mouth from hers and with the small distance that opened between their bodies he regained a measure of sanity. "Damn it. I didn't mean to hurt you." His voice sounded raw and rough-edged even to his own ears.

She took a quick, shuddering breath. "You didn't hurt me," she said, touching her fingers to her lips. "I'm fine." She didn't sound fine. She sounded as shook up as he was.

What had he been thinking? He barely knew this woman, even though their bodies reacted to each other as if they'd been lovers for years. "You've had a hell of a rough day and tomorrow will be an even tougher one. The last thing you need is to be pawed over."

"I was kind of enjoying it."

He was in no mood to make a joke of his lack of control. He slid his hands to her upper arms, holding her slightly away from him. He looked deep into her eyes, darkened by the night and emotion. "Even after what I suggested this afternoon, you're going to drive in the Sprint Cup race tomorrow?"

The softness left her glorious eyes, and her mouth thinned into a stubborn line. She wiggled free of his hands and scooted to the far side of the bench seat. Between one breath and the next, she had reverted to the warrior-goddess figure he'd seen that first day at Bristol. "I'll consider your advice, but I'm probably going to drive tomorrow."

Obviously he had been wrong about what lay hidden beneath her plastic media-darling overlay. What had happened to the softness she'd shown for the little boy with the mangled toes, her affection for her brothers and her family? Had he imagined those layers of her personality? Apparently he had. It was past time to get himself back in control, past time to remember that she was just as driven to succeed in her chosen career as Lisa had been—no matter the consequences, no matter the heartache. "Of course," he said, as angry with himself as he was disappointed in her. "I have no doubt you will do what you need to."

CHAPTER SEVEN

HE WAS ANGRY. Angry at himself, angry at her. Why? It had only been a kiss, after all. But what a kiss. It had curled her toes and took her breath away. She wanted to kiss him again to see if lightning would strike a second time when their lips met, but she knew he would rebuff her advances. Besides, her sexy public persona aside, she wasn't comfortable making advances to men, even a man like this one who rang all her bells and pushed all her buttons.

He levered himself out of the cart. He leaned forward so she could see his face beneath the hard vinyl top. "I don't usually kiss my patients." He cleared his throat. "In fact, I never do."

"Then I'll take it as a compliment."

"It was unprofessional behavior. I'll be happy to make you an appointment with another doctor."

"Are you saying you're unable to control your baser instincts around me, Dr. Abrams?" she asked, unable to keep from teasing him a little, perhaps because it helped defuse her own sexual tension and confusion a bit.

"Certainly not." He heard the pomposity in his own voice and laughed. "At least, I think I can."

"Then I see no reason for me not to keep my next appointment with you."

Did she really want to see him again? Be alone with him, even in a professional setting? Yes, she did. She was attracted to him, not as a physician or a healer, but as a man. That didn't happen to her often, and she wanted to see where the feelings led her. She wasn't going to get carried away; oh, no, she was too smart for that. But she had never backed down from a challenge—or her fears—and she wasn't about to start tonight.

"I don't think that's a good—"

"Why?" What was it about her that he didn't like? Whatever it was, it had nothing to do with his inability to keep his hands off a female patient. The thought of him violating his professional oath that way was ludicrous. No, whatever it was, it was personal. Maybe she reminded him of an old girlfriend? One that had broken his heart? It wouldn't be the first time that kind of thing had happened. She should probably just come out and ask him if that was the problem.

But then maybe he would say, "No, you're just not my type," and she didn't want that.

The door of the care center opened and a tall, lanky man with broad shoulders, a big nose and hands, and a head of wild-looking red hair stepped from the circle of light cast by the open door into the shadows that surrounded the cart.

"Matt, is that you?"

"Over here, Eagleson."

"Hey, bro, I thought you'd gone back to the motor home," he said, giving Kelsey a nod and a grin that was almost as broad as his shoulders. "Hi, there."

"Hi, yourself." Kelsey leaned her forearms on the steering wheel and smiled at the man she now recognized as the other doctor on duty in the care center.

She saw him raise his eyebrows, shaggy like his hair. "I'm not interrupting anything, am I?" he asked making a circling gesture between them.

"Yes," Matt growled.

"No," Kelsey contradicted. "We were just confirming my next appointment with Dr. Abrams."

"Kelsey—" Matt's tone held a warning note.

Kelsey's chin came up. Okay, maybe she'd read the signals wrong. Maybe he hadn't felt the same jolt of electricity that had coursed through her when their lips met, but she was damned if she was going to just slink away into the darkness and let these two males have a good laugh over her naïveté.

Would Matt do that? Kiss and tell? Maybe he would. After all, she barely knew him. And if she turned tail and ran, she never would. She stared straight forward out of the windshield of the Club Car so they couldn't see the heat she felt steal into her cheeks.

"Kelsey was just leaving," Matt said.

"Okay," Jamie said. "I think I'll go back inside. It's kind of cold out here without my jacket. See you later, Matt. Nice to meet you…Kelsey. That's your name, isn't it?" Jamie cocked his head and stared pointedly at his friend.

"Oh, hell, I didn't introduce you." Matt ground out the words. "Kelsey Kendall, Jamie Eagleson, until tonight my best friend."

Her instincts, her good old-fashioned feminine intuition, had been right. He'd been thrown off balance by that mind-blowing kiss just as badly as she had. She could see that now. Kelsey's spirits perked up. She turned her head and smiled at Matt's friend, "Nice to meet you, Dr. Eagleson."

"Jamie."

"Jamie." She smiled even more brightly and heard Matt grind his teeth.

"That was quite a roughing up you took today. I'm assuming my esteemed colleague is advising you to make an early night of it."

"Why, no, Doctor. He hasn't recommended any such thing."

Matt coughed and cleared his throat. "I concur with Dr. Eagleson's recommendation."

"Lord, Abrams, you sound like a pompous ass when you talk like that."

An overhead light was shining down on Matt's head and she saw his face flush. Suddenly she didn't want to tease him any more. She didn't want his friend to, either. She felt a little buzz along her nerve endings, like champagne bubbles in her blood. "I have every intention of doing exactly as you recommend just as soon as I drop Dr. Abrams off at the main gate."

"Then I won't keep you. Good night, Kelsey. 'Night, Matt. See you back at the motor home."

"Good night." They watched him reenter the care center in silence.

"Hop in," Kelsey said. She found herself holding her breath. What if he said yes? Would he kiss her again?

"No, thanks," he said pointing in the opposite direction, toward the VIP lot where her motor home was parked. "Go. Do as the good doctor ordered. Go to bed."

"What about you?"

"I'm going to walk."

Kelsey's heart dropped onto the floor of the golf cart.

"But you're not wearing a coat."

She could have bitten her tongue. What a ridiculous thing to say when you'd just gotten a brush-off.

His mouth quirked up into a lopsided grin, "Once a big sister, always a big sister."

Kelsey shrugged. "I can't seem to help myself." Her heart rebounded into her throat when his eyes fastened on her mouth and stayed there.

"Believe me," he said with a frown, directing his anger—or perhaps bemusement—inward, "I'm not in the least danger of cooling off, even if I walked all the way to Charlotte and back."

CHAPTER EIGHT

WHEELMAMA'S NASCAR blog:
Monday, March 29th, 2010.
9:28 a.m.
Posted from a campground in Martinsville:
Just passing along a few thoughts before packing up to head home to Mooresville after a hellofva' good weekend of racing here. Justin Murphy had a great day coming in a car length ahead of Bart Branch to claim the prized trophy in the NASCAR Sprint Cup race. Since I hear he and his wife are building a brand-new home on Lake Norman he'll have plenty of room to display his prize.

All of you know by now I'm not Kelsey Kendall's biggest fan but I have to admit she got up and drove the wheels off the No. 432 car yesterday. Despite the car not coming to her until late in the race, she never backed off the throttle. Heck of a run, girl, especially after taking a licking in a ten-car incident in the NASCAR Nationwide race on Saturday when she strapped in the GarTex Racing car to help out Casey Hilliard whose wife had a baby early Saturday morning—congrats Casey and LaDeena!

Twenty-second place isn't a bad finish. Good enough to keep Kelsey and PDQ Racing in the top 20. But you have to wonder what Jim Latimer thinks of her driving both races if she gets banged around like that again? Just a thought...

Still, if she keeps raking in the points over the next couple of months he probably will go along with it. I didn't think I'd be writing this but I can see Kelsey making a run at the Chase for the NASCAR Sprint Cup. If that happens I'd really have to eat crow. But I'm not worried yet. The girl's got game, but has she got what it takes to make it in the Show over the long haul? Rumor has it she spends most of her off time working out in a special room they set up at PDQ Racing just for her.

I know it ain't politically correct, but I don't care how many hours she spends liftin' weights, she ain't going to turn into Supergirl. I'm not going to get into it with youse guys on the boards about her record in open wheel. Open-wheel ain't NASCAR. My ninety-year-old Granny can drive an open-wheel car. Stock cars are a whole 'nother animal. Period. End of argument.

Keep your wheels on the ground 'til I get back to God's country.
WHEELMAMA

WHEELMAMA, THE NOM de plume of the blogger who had followed Kelsey to the clinic last week. Matt had taken to reading her postings when he had a minute or two to spare, especially if she was writing about Kelsey Kendall. In fact he'd done quite a bit of Internet surfing for information on the woman who was monopolizing most of his dreams and more than her fair share of his waking hours, too.

He skimmed the next week's blog entries but WHEEL-MAMA had stayed home and watched the Phoenix race on TV just as he had. Kelsey's engine had given out halfway through the race and she'd finished far back in the pack. He'd seen the post-race interview on one of the sports channels and she'd handled herself well—shrugging off her obvious disappointment, emphasizing the great pit stops her team had put together and vowing to make a better showing at Texas and Talladega, the next two races on the schedule.

Matt shut down his laptop and spun his desk chair around to face the window. Today the parking lot was bathed in early-April sunshine, and the temperature was in the eighties. It would have been a great day to head off to the beach or up into the mountains, but he had three post-op patients in recovery and two more surgeries scheduled for early the next morning. In fact, his surgery schedule was booked solid for the rest of the month. Today's consultation with Kelsey would be the last time he saw her for the foreseeable future.

The thought made him unusually restless. He stood up and paced around his desk. It was a quarter-past six. Kelsey was late for her appointment again. He scanned the parking lot. No van with an overweight female blogger or the media types in the SUV that had trailed Kelsey the first time they'd tried to discuss her case. Of course, there was no sleek black sports car out there either, only a beat-up old pickup that had seen better days.

"Doctor, Ms. Kendall is here to see you." It was his aunt at her most official. She opened the door of his office a little wider and stepped back. Kelsey, dressed in snug-fitting jeans and a cotton sweater the same sea-green color as her eyes, stepped over the threshold. She smiled at him and he thought for a moment the sun had returned to its midday brightness. Her hair, as sun-streaked as her smile, was pulled back into a ponytail. She didn't look old enough to even have a driver's license, let alone pilot a race car at speeds of 180 miles an hour.

"Here's her chart. Is there anything else I can get for you, Doctor?"

His aunt's unusual formality reminded him of his own professional responsibilities, restrictions that had been lacking from his nighttime fantasies and his daytime musings for the past couple of weeks or so. "Not right now, Mrs. Bartley. Thank you."

She hesitated a moment before nodding and leaving the room, not quite shutting the door behind her.

He was alone with Kelsey. He closed the chart he'd been pretending to study, bracing himself to look directly into those incredible green eyes of hers. Wham! Tsunami-force wave, just like in his dreams. He cleared his throat and held out his hand. "Sorry about what happened to your car yesterday."

She shrugged. "Crap happens. Mechanical failure's part of racing. We'll do better at Texas this week. And then Talladega's next up."

"Sounds like you're really looking forward to that one."

She grinned, spontaneous and unaffected, and he swallowed hard to keep from grinning back. "You bet I am."

He gestured to the chair in front of his desk. "Have a seat."

She sat down, her movements slower, less graceful than he remembered. She was in pain, he decided, although she would probably deny it if he called her on it. "I'm sorry I'm late. Traffic was fierce on the expressway."

"Just traffic?" he asked. "You didn't have to shake your media posse this time?"

"Just traffic. NASCAR drivers getting speeding tickets is frowned on. Bad for the image."

"Sexy, good. Irresponsible, not so good. I get it."

She relaxed a little, waved a hand in the air, "Exactly, Dr. Abrams." He wanted to say "Call me Matt," but didn't. Not now. Not here. Stick to business.

He walked around the desk and propped one hip on the corner. He picked up her chart and swiveled his computer screen so she could see the images of her spinal cord. "These are the MRI images we got," he said, making no mention of the first time he'd tried to discuss them with her. Quickly he explained what he saw on the films. "You do have the beginning stages of degenerative disc disease. It shouldn't interfere with your life for many years. If you're lucky, maybe never. But I stand by what I told you earlier. Driving a race car for a living is not a good option for you."

"I won't be forever. I can't quit yet," she said as quietly and as straightforwardly as he had spoken to her. "Not until I win a championship."

He felt anger churn inside him as she voiced her resistance, but he ignored it. She was his patient. Anger was not an option.

"You're in pain right now, aren't you?" he asked instead. She had driven over half of a five-hundred-mile race and made a four-hour plane flight back from Phoenix in the past twenty-four hours. If she said she wasn't hurting, she was lying to him, if not to herself.

She opened her mouth to deny his words. He was certain that's what she meant to do, but she surprised him. "Yes," she admitted, reaching up to touch her shoulder and the back of her neck. "But that doesn't change anything."

His blood ran cold in his veins. *Lisa.* He had hoped Kelsey was different, that when confronted with the undeniable facts she would prove more willing to listen to reason. Obviously he'd been wrong. She was still speaking, and he forced himself to let go of the hurt and the anger and listen to her.

"I...I was wondering if there was something we could do for the pain? I...I don't like to take drugs." She straightened in her chair. "In fact, I refuse to."

This was the old Kelsey, the fighter, the warrior princess of her hero cards. He'd picked up one at the racetrack in Bristol after their first encounter. It was in his desk drawer right now, sandwiched between a pair of old medical journals. He caught himself looking at it now and then, as starstruck as a thirteen-year-old boy.

"One thing that might help," he said, "is if you reduce your strength-conditioning routine."

"That's not an option," she said immediately. "One of the reasons there are so few women drivers in NASCAR is because of the amount of upper-body strength necessary to control a stock car going 180 miles an hour. I need all the advantage I can give myself."

"I thought that's what you'd say." He stuck his hands in the pocket of his lab coat so that he didn't reach out, take her by the shoulders and shake some sense into her. "All I'm suggesting is that you look into modifying your program to reduce the stress on your neck and upper vertebrae. Surely you can cooperate with me to that extent."

Her eyes darkened, narrowed. Once more he thought she would brush off his words, but again she surprised him. "I'll think about it." She lifted her hand to the back of her neck again, wincing slightly. "I do push myself in the gym," she confessed. "And my weight regimen is pretty intense."

"It's a start," he said, softening as he registered her anx-

iety. "And you might want to look into a course of thera-
peutic massage."

"I don't have time to go to the spa."

"It's not a beauty treatment. It's a form of physical ther-
apy." He found himself moving toward her, unable to stop
himself. "May I demonstrate?" he asked, positioning himself behind her chair.

She sat very straight, very still. "Yes, please."

He lifted his hands and saw they were shaking slightly,
the way they had been that first day at Bristol. She was a
patient. He couldn't let himself feel anything beyond professional concern. Not now. Not here. He placed his hands
on her shoulders, felt the soft brush of her ponytail against
his wrist and had to steel himself against the rush of heat.
Chemicals. Hormones. That was all. He could deal with it.

He hoped.

He began a slow, gentle massage of her upper back and
shoulders, the same movements he had performed for patients hundreds, if not thousands, of times in the years he'd
been in practice, but this was different. This was Kelsey, the
woman who possessed his thoughts and fueled his dreams
with images so erotic he woke aching. When he was with
her, he didn't feel like a healer; he felt like a man who was
very much attracted to the woman he was touching.

She sighed very softly, a whisper of sound, no more.
He felt her pain-tightened muscles begin to relax beneath
his touch. "That feels better already," she said, turning
her head so that the end of her ponytail wrapped itself
around his wrist, holding him captive with silken cords. He
leaned forward slightly. She smelled good, lily of the valley
or something equally old-fashioned and feminine. The
warmth of her skin seeped into his muscle fibers, inflamed

his nerves and roiled his imagination. "That feels so good. Don't stop, please."

Alarms went off in his brain. Her words didn't register as those of a grateful patient, but of a desirable woman. He should stop now, walk over to his desk, inform her he couldn't treat her any longer because he wanted to do all kinds of things with her, and to her, that an ethical physician could never do.

Instead he leaned forward and touched his mouth to hers. She didn't move, didn't pull away, but just for a moment she hesitated. He got hold of himself, began to straighten up, to pull away, but she reached up and touched his cheek and he was lost all over again. He tightened his grip on her shoulders and kissed her long and deep, and she kissed him back.

"Good heavens, Matt... I mean, Dr. Abrams, what's going on here?"

"Is she gone?" Matt stayed in the shadows of an unused exam room doorway and spoke to his aunt's back. She was sitting at the reception desk, tapping away at the computer, double-checking his surgery schedule for the following morning just like she always did the last thing before she left each day.

"Of course she's gone. You didn't expect her to hang around after you behaved the way you did?" she asked without turning around. They were alone. She wasn't his nurse/office manager now; she was his aunt, his mother's twin sister. Although the two women weren't identical twins, the resemblance was close enough to make him uneasy when Darla resorted to that don't-try-to-con-me tone.

He shoved his hand through his hair. "I don't have any excuses for my behavior."

She waved off his stiff protest. "Oh, don't be silly. You're attracted to her, aren't you?"

"Yes," he said. There was no use lying to her, she knew him too well for that.

She nodded, "Thought so. Even broken hearts heal eventually. It was bound to happen again sooner or later—not in an office setting, of course, that's not good. But—" She threw up her hands in frustration. "You know what I mean."

"She's not my type," he said.

"From the looks of that lip-lock, she most definitely is your type." She swiveled her chair to face him. "You don't believe all those things you read about her in the media are true? That she's a party girl. NASCAR's siren, all that silliness?" She tilted her head and gave him a skeptical look.

"No, I don't believe all the hype."

"Well, thank goodness for that bit of sense. Let's see, what else could it be? She's pretty and she's spirited and she has a job most men would give their left arm to have." Her lips thinned, and she became serious. "Oh, dear, that's it, isn't it? It's her job."

He opened his mouth to protest, but nothing came out.

"Oh, not that she's a race-car driver, but that she's a determined and successful one, with her eye on a NASCAR championship in the future."

"How do you know all that about her?" he asked, hoping to distract her from the large kernel of truth in her words, and knowing he would fail.

"I told you, I'm a fan. But that doesn't make her another Lisa," she said.

"Doesn't it? How do you know on the basis of a fifteen-minute acquaintance and a bunch of blog entries?"

"Point taken." She shrugged and turned back to her work. "Okay, lecture over. You'll have to figure this out on your own. I have just one more thing to say on the subject of Kelsey Kendall. I'm a pretty good judge of character. I think she's good people."

"You never said that about Lisa."

She remained silent.

"Point taken."

"I just hope she follows through with Dr. Fujika."

He turned to head back to his office. Now that Kelsey was gone he could return to his lair. "What do you mean by that?"

"I don't have to be a NASCAR expert to figure out that any sign of weakness brings out the sharks. She's already being hounded by the media. Remember, you told me that yourself when she got that cinder in her eye at Bristol. If they catch her going into another doctor's office…"

"Damn." He hadn't thought of that, before but it was crystal clear now. She would blow off the appointment with Fujika, go back to her regular routine and someday she'd pay the price and it would be his fault. "Now what do I do?"

Again silence from his aunt. She wasn't going to make this easy for him.

"All right," he surrendered. "If she doesn't keep her appointment with Fujika, I'll track her down and try and talk some sense into her. Does that work for you?"

"It's a start."

CHAPTER NINE

THE SUN HAD DIPPED below the horizon and the spring twilight was fading into darkness as Matt drove up to the small bungalow-style house where Kelsey lived on a tree-lined street on the outskirts of Mooresville. He'd let a week go by before he'd called Dr. Fujika to see if Kelsey had kept her promise to see him. According to his receptionist, she had no record of her even making an appointment. Now it was up to him to follow through on his promise to his aunt to find out why she had gone back on her word.

He knew he could have done this over the phone. He had her cell number on a slip of paper in his pocket, but for some reason that seemed to him to be the coward's way out. He wanted to make sure she was getting the medical help she needed, but damn it, he also wanted to see her again, too. He couldn't help himself. And while he was at it, he supposed he would have to apologize for kissing her in his office. The trouble was, he didn't want to apologize. He wanted to repeat the offense.

He switched off the ignition and got out of the car. The house had a wide front porch deep enough to accommodate an old-fashioned wicker porch swing hanging from the ceiling by metal chains, and two matching wicker chairs. He thought about sitting in that swing on quiet summer nights, Kelsey beside him, his arm around her—kissing her.

A light was burning in one of the windows that flanked the door. There was light behind its glass insert, as well. He lifted his hand to ring the bell. Chimes sounded somewhere inside and a moment later a voice called out, "I'll be right there." *Kelsey's voice.* The sound of it raised the short hairs on the back of his neck, sent blood rushing through his body.

The door opened. Her mouth dropped open. She recovered quickly and shut it again. "Matt? What are you doing here? How did you find out where I live?" She didn't smile. He had hoped she might favor him with one but wasn't surprised that she didn't. At least she didn't refer to him by his title. He decided to take that as a good sign.

"Your address was on your chart in my office. I...I came to see why you didn't make an appointment with Dr. Fujika. And I guess I came to apologize for taking advantage of you in my office that day," he added hastily. He had to stop himself from lifting his hand to rake it through his hair. Instead, he shoved both of them into the pockets of his jacket. "That was a damned unprofessional thing to do."

Her expression was guarded, but he saw a hint of laughter behind the initial wariness in her eyes. She made a shooing motion with her hand and he stepped back from the screen. She opened it and came outside. "I'd invite you in but the place is a mess," she said candidly. "I'm just leaving for the airport. We have to be wheels up for Dallas/Fort Worth in less than an hour."

"The race isn't until Sunday. This is only Thursday." He let his eyes drift slightly lower to the soft redness of her mouth. That was a mistake. All he could think about now was how warm and pliant it had been beneath his.

"I have sponsor obligations," she said. He dragged his gaze away from her mouth and tried to focus on some part of her that didn't set his heart hammering in his chest. It wasn't easy. She was wearing a soft silky-looking, rose-colored tunic over a slim black skirt. The tunic was belted tight around her waist and was only a couple of inches shorter than the skirt. He'd had no idea she had such long legs. They seemed to go on forever and ended in a pair of stiletto-heeled black pumps. Wearing those shoes, she was almost as tall as he was. Her eyes were on a level with his, her mouth, too. Her hair was loose on her shoulders and big gold hoops swung from her ears. A trio of gold chains nestled above the low-scooped neckline of her top. Matt swallowed hard. She had been sexy as hell in her figure-hugging uniform, but tonight… Tonight she was all female, all woman, and she took his breath away.

"I told you before you didn't need to apologize for kissing me. I liked it. I told you that, too. You were just so shook up it must not have registered."

"I wasn't shook up."

She raised one arched eyebrow and tilted her head, just a hint of her incredible smile playing at the corners of her mouth. "Are you sure you weren't just a tiny bit shook up? I certainly was."

He hadn't expected her to react this way. He'd braced himself for her anger, for her to be cool and standoffish; after all, he'd not only embarrassed himself, he'd embarrassed her in front of his aunt. Instead, she'd stood the whole scenario on its head. He was out of his depth, and they both knew it. "You were?"

"I've never been kissed by my doctor like that before."

"I hope to hell you never are again," he growled before he could stop himself.

She pushed out her lower lip in a little pout. "I'm not sure I agree with you there."

Matt cleared his throat, fought to regain control of himself. "Regardless, I apologize."

"Accepted. Now we're even. No need for more apologies on either side." The teasing glint left her eyes. He wished he could bring it back but he didn't know how. He wasn't good at this give-and-take between a man and a woman. He never had been. "You can go back to your condo in Concord and stop worrying about me and my aches and pains."

"No, I can't," he said stubbornly. "Not until I find out why you didn't follow through with an appointment with Dr. Fujika."

She blew out an exasperated breath. "What makes you think I didn't make an appointment with his office?"

He could hear a car coming down the street. Her eyes flicked past his shoulder and he knew it was her ride to the airport pulling up. Damn, no time to take this conversation any further. He had only a minute or two to convince her to take his advice.

"I called and asked," he said. "They didn't have any appointment listed for you."

"Because I didn't make one under my own name," she said with exaggerated patience, as though she were speaking to someone who was not very bright. "I made it under my grandmother's name, Margaret Kelsey."

"You were named for your grandmother?" he asked, knowing he sounded like the fool she must think him.

"It's a fine old Southern tradition, giving a child their grandmother's maiden name." A car door slammed. She waved at whoever had gotten out of the car. "Look, my ride's here. Is that all you wanted to know? That I kept my appointment? You can rest easy. I followed through on your recommendation. Dr. Fujika concurred with your assessment. I'm modifying my weight-training regime and I've already had a couple of massage-therapy sessions. You don't have to feel responsible for me anymore, okay? You'll understand if I don't say I hope I see you around the track." She gave him one of her blinding plastic smiles, but it never reached her eyes.

"No, Kelsey, damn it. I—" What did he want? He wanted to kiss her again but there was more to it than that. He could have handled the merely physical. He could have worked her out of his system if that was all there was to it.

But there was more. He wanted to spend time with her, to learn all there was to know about her, to trust his aunt's instincts and his own that she was not the kind of woman Lisa had been.

"What?" she asked, and he took courage from the hopeful note in her voice.

"I want to—"

"Kelsey, are you ready to roll?" A man's voice came from directly behind him. Kelsey's eyes darted upward and a little frown pulled her eyebrows together for a moment before she smiled and nodded. "I'm ready, Jake."

"Who's this?"

Matt swiveled his head to find himself looking at the Adam's apple of a guy who stood half a head taller than his own six feet.

"Dr. Matt Abrams, my brother, Deputy Jake Kendall." Dressed all in black with a service revolver at his side, Kelsey's brother was a formidable sight.

The cop held out his hand. "Doc."

"Deputy." The guy was the size of a mountain. He out-weighed Matt by fifty pounds, and his handshake resembled a vise grip.

"Ready to go, sis? I have to be back on duty by eight."

"All ready." Kelsey reached back into the house and grabbed a canvas duffel. "Take this to the car, will you?"

"That's all the luggage you have?"

"Already sent it ahead to be loaded on the plane," she informed them. "That's my favorite helmet. I don't trust anyone else with it. Be careful putting it in the car."

"Nice to meet you, Doc," the hulking deputy said, but he didn't sound as if he meant it. He gave Matt one more long, hard look and turned, reluctantly, back toward his car.

"Big brother," Kelsey said, as if that explained the cop's wariness toward him. Matt supposed it did.

"I'll say. Are all your brothers that size?"

"Pretty much." She stepped back inside the house to switch off the lights and grabbed a sexy little black purse from a hook beside the door. She pulled the front door shut, and Matt heard the lock snap into place. She wrapped her hands around the purse and faced him once more. "You were going to say something before my brother interrupted—"

"I—" The cop was standing with his shoulder leaning against the roof of his squad car. Matt could feel his eyes boring a hole between his shoulder blades. *I what? Want you? Desire you? Maybe I'm even starting to fall in love with you.*

The admission sent cold shivers up and down his spine. *In love.* He didn't want to be that vulnerable again. Not in this lifetime.

"Matt, I have to go."

"Yeah, me, too," he held out his hand. "I just wanted to wish you great racing."

JAMIE CLICKED THE REMOTE and the big-screen TV went dark. He stood up from the overstuffed couch and stretched and yawned. "Seventh-place finish. Not bad. Not bad at all. Top twenty last week at Texas, top ten this week at 'Dega. Your girl's on the move."

Matt tightened his jaw and took a pull on his beer. It was warm. He grimaced but didn't let Jamie goad him into a reply.

His friend ignored his silence and went on talking, "Glad we didn't draw that infield duty, though. Four cars out in the same accident."

But not Kelsey. She had been ahead of the pack that was taken out.

"And nothing worse for any of the drivers to show for all that mayhem other than a sprained wrist and some bumps and bruises." Jamie shook his head, "Fricking amazing."

"She drove a good race." Matt continued to stare at the blank screen following his own line of thought. The ghostly image of Kelsey, flushed and laughing as she traded high fives with her teammates, remained burned on his retina.

"Drove good and looks good. Relaxed, loose. Damned sexy, too."

"What?" Matt's head snapped up. He scowled at his friend.

Jamie grinned. "Thought that might get your attention. You going to sit there all night staring at nothing?" Jamie inquired. "If you are, I'm heading out. I'm playing golf in the morning. Early tee time. Want to come along? It's just a pick-up game."

"Nope, can't make it. Early office hours tomorrow." He wondered what Kelsey was doing now. Would she be having dinner with her teammates to celebrate the top-ten finish? Or would she already be headed for the airport for the flight back to Mooresville?

"Why don't you call her and congratulate her?" Jamie

suggested, reading his mind. "I know you've still got her cell number in your wallet."

"Not a good idea."

"Why not? You've signed off her case. There's no more ethical conflict. Don't try to deny it you've got it bad for her."

"I'll get over it."

"Why do you want to get over it?"

"It wouldn't work."

Jamie blew out an exasperated breath. "It's too late for this same-old, same-old argument again. I've only got one thing more to say and then I'm out of here."

"What's that?"

"She's not Lisa, man. Get over it."

CHAPTER TEN

"KELSEY! IT'S GOOD to see you. It's been ages since you've joined the gang. Come over here. There's someone I want you to meet." Sophia Grosso Murphy, glowingly happy, stood up from a comfy, overstuffed chair, one of several that had found its way into the back room of Maudie's Down Home Diner, where the Tuesday Tarts met.

Tuesday Tarts. The name, politically incorrect as it might be in some circles, always made Kelsey smile when she heard it applied to the loose association of NASCAR wives and mothers that made up the group. Most of them were of her mother and grandmother's generation but lately the group had been attracting a younger crowd, thanks mainly to Sophia and her friends.

The room where the Tarts met was half storage area, half cozy sitting room, created after a kitchen renovation years before. It was a down-home NASCAR nation version of an upscale-restaurant's chef's table, Kelsey had decided after her first visit. The excellent food and good company kept her coming back. She was comfortable in their sisterhood and able to be herself. She valued the time she spent with them. She looked around the white-covered tables where half a dozen women sat eating salads and drinking coffee and sweet tea. She poured herself a glass of iced tea and smiled at the young woman seated beside her friend.

"Kelsey, this is Daisy Brookshire. She's working for Rue Larrabee at Cut 'N' Chat now. You'll love her work. Look what she did for this mop of mine." Sophia tilted her head so that Kelsey could get the full effect of her new softer, sleeker style.

"Hi, Daisy. It's nice to meet you."

"It's nice to meet you, too."

Kelsey studied Sophia's new haircut. "That's a good look for you."

"Daisy will do wonders for your hair, too."

"I'm sure she would," Kelsey said carefully.

"I don't imagine you'd want something that short when you're driving, though," Daisy said with a quick mischievous grin that came and went in a heartbeat.

Kelsey laughed. "You read my mind. I'd have the worst case of helmet hair you've ever seen after a race if mine was that short. But I could use a trim. Are you taking new clients?"

Daisy looked pleased. "I'd be happy to have you."

"I'm recommending her to all my friends." Sophia said, "So don't wait too long or she'll be too booked to fit you into her schedule."

"I'm not that busy," Daisy said. "Now if ya'll will excuse me, my next appointment is due in a few minutes and I need to get back to the salon. Thanks for inviting me this evening, Sophia."

Silence reigned for a minute or two after Daisy left the room.

"Poor kid," Sophia said shaking her head. "And her poor little one. It's so sad to think the baby will never know its daddy."

Sophia handed Kelsey a plate with two jam tarts and what appeared to be a mini chocolate cream puff. Sophia knew she had a weak spot for chocolate.

"She's pregnant? I didn't notice."

Sophia nodded. "She's due in the fall."

"What happened to her baby's father?"

"He was killed in a freak paragliding accident in the Bahamas. Can you imagine that?"

"How terrible," Kelsey said.

"Yes, and now his parents are trying to coerce that poor sweet girl into giving them her baby."

Kelsey's mouth was full, but she raised her eyebrows to encourage Sophia to go on.

"She's a nervous wreck about it all. The grandparents are rolling in money. Daisy's family doesn't have any money to spare, and besides, they're all in Florida."

"Sounds like she could use some help." Kelsey couldn't imagine being alone in the world. Her parents, her brothers, no matter how exasperating they could be, would always be there for her if she needed them—and she would always be there for them. That was what family was all about.

Sophia sighed. "I've offered but she won't let me loan her money for a lawyer. I think she's hoping if she lays low it will all just go away, but Nana says August Carlyle is a mean old coot and when he wants something, he'll ride roughshod over whoever stands in his way."

"Let me know if there's anything I can do."

"Well, letting her work on that glorious mane of yours is a start."

"I can do that."

"And leave a very generous tip, will you? She's squirreling away every cent she can get her hands on."

"I'll do that, too. Now what else is going on around here?"

"I'm waiting for Mom and Nana to join me for dinner. It's poker night at the Farm. The guys are ordering in pizza and barbecue. You'll stay and eat with us, won't you? We haven't seen you for weeks."

"I've been busy."

"I know, I know. I didn't get a chance yet to congratulate you on two pretty good finishes. Inside the top twenty at Texas and seventh at Talladega! Not bad for your rookie season, girl."

"I had good cars and my guys are working together like they're controlled by one brain."

"You've got one of the best crew chiefs in the business," Sophia said.

"Amen."

"But we're going short-track racing this week," Sophia said. She could be intuitive when she set her mind to it. "And you're remembering Bristol and Martinsville."

"Short track's not my forte, that's for sure."

"It will be this week. Justin was telling me just the other night that he's noticed a big improvement in your driving. He says he's beginning to dread seeing you come up in his rearview mirror."

Kelsey felt a faint flush creep into her cheeks. Justin Murphy was contending for the Chase for the NASCAR Sprint Cup this season. If he was beginning to think of her as a driver to be reckoned with, she really must be showing improvement. "That's quite a compliment coming from your husband."

"I know it is." Sophia looked over her shoulder and raised her hand. "Mom and Nana are here."

"Hello, Kelsey," Patsy Grosso said, bending to give her

daughter a peck on the cheek. "How's my sweet daughter doing?" she asked, smiling a greeting in Kelsey's direction.

"Starving," Sophia replied. "Hi, Nana. How's Milo feeling?" Sophia's great-grandfather, Milo Grosso, one of the last of the founding generation of NASCAR drivers and a former FBI agent, was in his nineties but still a force to be reckoned with.

"Much better. His cold is nearly gone. We've decided to go to Richmond this weekend. Hi, honey, glad to see you here." Juliana wrapped her ample arms around Kelsey and gave her a quick hug. "Congratulations on your last two finishes. You're doing the Tarts proud."

"Thanks, Nana."

"Are you joining us for dinner, or are you dining with that hunky M.D. I saw sitting at the counter?"

"I…I'm not meeting anyone," Kelsey said. She had come through the kitchen entrance because it was raining and the only parking spot she could find was on that side of the building. She hadn't even glanced into the main room of the diner. Could Juliana's hunky M.D. be Matt? Her heart beat a little faster. She hadn't seen or heard from him for almost two weeks, not since the night he'd stopped by her house. She thought by now she would be over thinking about him, but far from it. He was on her mind, or lingering just on the edge of her thoughts, every waking hour she wasn't behind the wheel of her race car.

And the nights. The nights were the worst. He was the subject of every dream she had, and some of them had been very, very explicit indeed. She felt her face grow hot just thinking about them.

"Do you know who he is?" Sophia asked, her sharp eyes not missing the flush that suffused Kelsey's cheeks.

"Of course. I'm not in the habit of making conversation with strange men, Sophia. It's Dr. Matt Abrams," Juliana confirmed. "I recognized him the moment I saw him. Milo consulted him when his knees were bothering him last winter. He remembered me and was kind enough to inquire about Milo's condition. I told him he was doing well."

"He's sitting at the counter beside Bart Branch." Patsy supplied. "They're both talking to that pretty new waitress. What's her name? Mellie?"

Sophia's eyes widened and she exchanged a glance with her great-grandmother. "Gossip around the garages is that Bart's pretty much a fixture on that stool these days, and I don't think it's because he can't get enough of Sheila's meat-loaf sandwiches."

"Is that so?" Juliana said, looking over her shoulder.

"Nana," Patsy said, shaking a finger at the older woman. "No matchmaking."

"The thought never crossed my mind."

Patsy laughed. "Tell me another one," she said as she poured Juliana a glass of sweet tea.

"I wonder how Dr. Abrams found his way out here to Maudie's?" Juliana mused.

"I brought him," Kelsey said. She had nothing to hide. Sheila Trueblood, and who knew how many other people, had seen her with him that first night.

"You?" Sophia's mouth fell open in surprise. All the Tarts were aware that Kelsey's sexy party-girl public persona didn't carry over into her personal life. "Where did you meet him?"

"At Bristol. He was one of the doctors in the care center. And…again at Martinsville when I got caught in that pileup in the Nationwide race." No need to say anything about her back problems. She trusted the Grosso women, but she was all too aware that other ears were listening in.

"He did my friend's hip replacement last winter. She's the one that recommended Milo see him. She's still half in love with him." Juliana's eyes narrowed as she pinned Kelsey back in her chair with a piercing gaze. "Is he the mysterious man in the golf cart?"

"What?" Patsy demanded. "What are you talking about, Nana?"

"I think perhaps we should let Kelsey give us the details," Juliana said.

Kelsey groaned under her breath. Juliana knew everything, absolutely everything, that went on behind the scenes in NASCAR. She had for over fifty years. And worse, she was a matchmaker from way back. Her blue eyes began to shine with the excitement of a new romantic challenge in the offing.

Sophia whispered, "He's the man in the golf cart. The one you were kissing. I heard the gossip going around the garages, well, Justin did, but I didn't believe it."

Kelsey groaned and wished she could slide under the table and disappear. "It was just a kiss."

"Must have been some kiss if he's here looking for you," Sophia declared, clasping her hands over her heart. "Go. Go to him."

"He's not here looking for me," Kelsey said firmly. "We aren't seeing each other."

"Professionally," Sophia said. "Don't split hairs with me."

"Neither professionally nor personally. We…he…isn't my type." She waited for the heavenly thunderclap to break over her head. She was a liar and not a very good one, judging from the looks on the Grosso women's faces.

"Honey, a man like that is every woman's type," Juliana said as Sheila came through the swinging door from the kitchen.

"What man?" Sheila asked, looking curious. "Hi, Kelsey. I didn't see you come in."

"Hi, Sheila," Kelsey said, feeling a little faint.

"Kelsey's sexy doctor friend," Sophia enlightened the diner owner. "He's sitting at the counter with Bart Branch."

Sheila blew out an appreciative breath as she set a plate of cheese and crackers in front of Sophia. "That one. Newest regular. He's in here almost as often as Bart Branch." She snapped her fingers, zeroed in on Kelsey's face. "Now I remember. You came in here together a couple of weeks ago. Congratulations."

"He's not—" Kelsey attempted but couldn't get the words past the sudden tightening in her throat. She couldn't lie to herself any more than she could lie to her friends. She was very, very interested in Matt Abrams, and not in a doctor-patient way.

"He was at the register paying his tab as I walked in here. I'll see if I can catch him."

"No!"

"Don't you want him to know you're here?" She glanced around the table seeking enlightenment.

"Yes. No. I don't know," Kelsey finished miserably. Could she go after him? What if he was only here for the meat-loaf sandwiches? Then what would she do?

Juliana made up her mind for her. "Well, for heaven's sake, girl, don't just sit there dithering. Go after him."

CHAPTER ELEVEN

"Go through the kitchen," Sophia hissed, making shooing motions with her hands. "Catch him in the parking lot. Hurry!"

Kelsey began to move, responding as much to the urgency in her heart as the commanding note in her friend's voice. She pushed open the swinging door and slipped out the way she had come in, through the brightly lit kitchen, ignoring the curious glances of the two cooks.

The rain had stopped, at least for the moment. Off in the distance, she heard a rumble of thunder. Spring had come to Mooresville over the past couple of weeks and she'd been too busy, too preoccupied with her racing and her midnight dreams of making love to Matt, to notice. The small parking lot that paralleled the diner held a couple dozen cars. She had no idea what kind of vehicle Matt drove. He might not even have parked here, but across the street or down the block.

Her steps faltered and slowed. She had missed him somehow; she had lost her chance. It began to rain again. She turned up the collar of her raincoat and started for her car. She couldn't retreat inside the diner, slink back to her friends, admit she didn't have the courage to fight for the man she…was attracted to—that was as far as she could go with that line of thought. She couldn't even begin to think the L word, not yet. Probably never. The realization hurt enough to make her wince.

Footsteps sounded on the gravel behind her. She turned her head to see Matt approaching around the corner from the front of the building. His hands were shoved into the pockets of his leather jacket. His head was bowed against the increasingly heavy rainfall. He didn't see her until they were only a few steps apart.

"Hello, Matt," she said, pleased that her voice hadn't betrayed the sudden flare of desire the sight of him produced deep inside her.

"Kelsey?" He raised his head, his expression hovering somewhere between a frown and a smile when he caught sight of her.

"I didn't expect to run into you here," she said. That was the truth, so she didn't have too much trouble getting the words past the tightening in her throat caused by his sudden proximity and the incredibly alluring smell of rain, wet leather and the woodsy scent of his aftershave.

"I came for a meat-loaf sandwich," he said, smiling. "I've developed a real fondness for them." Kelsey caught her breath and smiled back as he moved closer, half turning to shield her from the windblown rain.

Thunder boomed again, closer this time, and lightning zigzagged across the storm-darkened sky. She liked thunderstorms as a rule, but this one was threatening to put an end to their conversation before she was ready. "The meat-loaf sandwiches at Maudie's have been known to lure men from farther away than Concord."

"I was also hoping to see you," he said.

Her heart galloped away in her chest. "Why?" she asked softly.

"To congratulate you on your finish at Talladega and to ask how you're feeling."

It wasn't precisely what she'd wanted to hear but had she really expected him to confess that he had haunted Maudie's front counter every night because he couldn't live without seeing her again? She almost smiled at the hokey image of Matt pining away for her—especially with half a pound of meat loaf on a plate in front of him. But it was a beginning. She didn't intend to let the opportunity slip away. "You watched the race?"

"Both of them."

Another flare of lightning gave her a quick glimpse of his face, of the shuttered look in his dark eyes. She might have lost her nerve if she also hadn't seen his pulse beating strong and fast in his throat.

Kelsey experienced momentary panic. He had the look of a man who was getting ready to say, "It's been good talking to you. See you around sometime."

She didn't want him to go. But was she ready to ask him back to her house? Was she ready to take that step? If she didn't make the effort, she knew deep inside she would regret it for the rest of her life. The storm had moved closer while they talked. Kelsey took a deep breath, took the plunge. "We can't stay here," she said as lightning flashed directly overhead.

He looked up at the dark sky as if noticing the storm for the first time. "I'd better go. I don't want to keep you standing out in the storm." He didn't make any move to walk away.

Kelsey felt the silent urging of the women she'd left behind. She heard Sophia's voice, plain as day. *"Don't lose your nerve."*

Patsy counseled, *"Take the initiative."*

But it was Juliana's command that echoed most loudly in her ears and her heart. *"Don't let him get away."*

"Would you like to come to my place for coffee or a glass of wine?"

He looked down at the ground, then met her eyes, his expression guarded, not giving his thoughts away. "I'd like that," he said at last.

Kelsey hadn't realized she'd been holding her breath until she opened her mouth to speak. "Follow me," she said and headed for her car before either of them could change their minds.

MATT TRAILED THE RED taillights of Kelsey's shiny black car through the pouring rain. She wasn't hard to keep up with, and he knew the way. He was no more than a few car lengths behind her when she pulled her sleek little black car around to the back of the small stone-and-timber bungalow and signaled he should do the same. She slipped out of the car, a black trench coat hugging her curves, her long golden hair glistening with moisture as she waited for him to get out of his SUV.

"Will your brother be all right with me parking back here?" he asked as she led the way up a flagstone path to a small enclosed back porch.

She laughed. "He'd better be. He knows I don't appreciate him checking up on me."

"He didn't seem all that impressed with me that night I stopped by."

"He's never impressed with my…with my male friends."

The small talk got them through the ritual of unlocking the door and turning on lights. He followed Kelsey across the threshold and into a long narrow kitchen, with old-fashioned appliances, white-painted cupboards and age-darkened pine floors that extended the length of the house. A half wall was topped by a counter that opened onto a view of the living room and its fieldstone fireplace. Off to the left, a hallway led to bedrooms and bathrooms. The front porch he'd noted on his first visit would be a great place to sit on summer evenings and watch the sun go down. He couldn't remember the last time he'd sat on a porch swing and watched the sunset. The idea of doing just that with Kelsey beside him held great appeal.

"Would you like something to drink?" she asked, hanging her coat on a hook by the door.

"A beer, if you've got it." Tomorrow was Wednesday. He didn't have office hours until one. He could indulge in a beer or two along with his fantasies of rocking in the porch swing with Kelsey.

"Coming right up. I think I can scrounge up some cheese and crackers, too, if you're still hungry."

"I'm good."

"Well, I'm starving," she said. "Wish I had something more substantial but I'm away so much during the race season that I don't keep much food on hand. Now, if we were in my motor home…well, let's just say my driver is one heck of a good cook."

"Do you like being on the move so much?"

He saw her stiffen slightly and wondered why his question had upset her. It seemed logical to ask. Had he somehow let his bitterness toward Lisa seep into his voice? He honestly hadn't been thinking about his ex-fiancée, hadn't for quite a while now. The realization didn't surprise him as much as it should have. It was time to move on, just as Jamie had said.

He wanted to make that move into a new future with
Kelsey. He'd realized that with his heart, if not with his
rational brain, days ago. It was why he'd spent so much
time at Maudie's these past two weeks—hoping he'd run
into Kelsey. That, and the meat-loaf sandwiches.

"Here you go," she said, bringing him a bottle of beer.
She held a plate of cheese and crackers in her other hand.
"Take this over by the fireplace and I'll get myself a diet
soda."

"You're not drinking?"

"No," she said, rolling her eyes. "I gained two pounds.
Male drivers might get away with a little spare tire underneath their uniforms. I never will." She laughed as she
sank down cross-legged onto the rug in front of the fireplace. He dropped down beside her, his back to the couch.
"I can see the look on your face," she said, waving a finger
at him. "You're wondering if I'm one of those women who
starves herself for the sake of her image. You couldn't be
more wrong. I'm saving myself for Friday night, that's all.
I'm taking my whole team to this hole-in-the-wall place
about twenty miles from the track. The catfish and fried dill
pickles are to die for."

"Fried dill pickles?"

"You haven't lived 'til you've had deep-fried dill pickles."

"I'll take your word for it. Nice place you've got here,"
he said as she chose a cracker, placed a square of cheese
on it and popped it into her mouth.

"Thanks."

She pushed the plate of food in his direction so she
wouldn't be tempted to eat more, he thought, hiding a grin.

"I like it," Kelsey said. "The location is great. I'm going

to add on to it someday, finish the upstairs, upgrade the kitchen and bathroom, add a hot tub to soak in on cold winter nights."

"I like your ideas for this place."

Matt thought about his condo in Charlotte—off-white walls and neutral furniture, and a view of two chain restaurants and an all-night check-cashing store from the postage-stamp-size balcony. He and Lisa had chosen it mainly for its location halfway between his clinic and the hospital where she was in residency. It had never really seemed like home even before their breakup.

"I've got the money saved up," Kelsey said, pulling one of the couch cushions down behind her back and inviting him to do the same. "Now all I need is the time."

"That's my problem, too."

She slipped off her sandals and crossed her slim legs at the ankles. After a moment's hesitation, he toed off his shoes and found her smiling at him when he turned his head. "There, now we can be comfortable." And he was comfortable, at least on one level. On another, he felt as if his nerve endings were connected to battery wires.

"All we need is a fire," he said.

"I can manage that." She picked up a remote from the end table and pushed a button. "Gas," she said. "No muss. No fuss. I hate cleaning out ashes."

"Nice." He propped one arm behind his head and watched the flames dancing among the ceramic logs.

"It is nice."

She set her glass on the end table, crossed her arms on her slender stomach and stared at the flames. She was wearing a cotton sweater in a honey-gold shade that echoed the gold in her hair and eyelashes. He curled his hand into a fist to keep from giving in to the desire to take her into his arms and hold her close.

They watched the flames in silence. He struggled with his doubts and fears, but the hunger for her was stronger than the memories of old hurts. Keeping away from her for these past days, trying to talk himself out of desiring her, needing her, hadn't worked. He was ready to move on. He was ready to let love back into his life. He wanted to share that life with Kelsey. He set his empty beer bottle on the floor and turned to take her in his arms and tell her so.

"Kelsey."

He didn't get any further with his declaration, or his lovemaking. The woman he was on the verge of falling in love with was already fast asleep.

CHAPTER TWELVE

KELSEY CUDDLED CLOSER to the warmth that enveloped her. She floated halfway between waking and sleeping and let herself believe the dream she'd been having was real. It wasn't an elaborate fantasy, but one very close to her heart. She had found her soul mate, her true love. They were together, and always would be, lovers and partners.

She sighed, keeping her eyes tight shut to hold in the dream, still reluctant to fully wake, but daylight beckoned beyond her closed eyelids. She had a lot to do.

She opened her eyes but one element of her fantasy didn't end. The heavy weight of a man's arm across her body was still there, still holding her close and safe. She stiffened momentarily, then turned slowly to find Matt staring back at her. They were lying on the couch pillows in front of the fireplace. Sometime during the night he had taken the heavy woven throw off the back of the sofa and covered them with it.

"You've been here all night?" she asked, not sure what to do next—stay where she was, or scoot out from under his warm, heavy hand and put some distance between them.

"You asked me to stay."

"I did?"

"You wouldn't take 'no' for an answer."

She felt herself blush. He smiled at her confusion, and her heart skipped a couple of beats. He was a good-looking man, but she had never seen him this way before, his hair tousled, stubble darkening his chin. He looked rested and alert and very, very sexy. "I…I must have been talking in my sleep."

"Maybe," he said, smiling again, "but you didn't seem inclined to let go of my hand."

She closed her eyes in mortification. She hadn't been dreaming. She had really asked him to stay and sleep beside her, and he had. What would he think of her now? That she really was the kind of woman the tabloids and the publicists made her out to be?

He brushed his finger across her chin, urging her to open her eyes. "I stayed because I wanted to, Kelsey," he said quietly. He lowered his head and kissed her, softly at first, but when she opened her mouth beneath his, he shifted his weight and pulled her into his arms, deepening the kiss, claiming her. She wound her arms around his neck and kissed him back, branding him with her own passionate response.

His hands brushed across her body, skimmed over her hips and bottom, pressed her tight against him. The kiss went on forever, and then was over much too quickly. They stayed side by side, hearts beating in rhythm, neither moving to take the intimacies further, but both reluctant to move apart.

"You kiss damned good," he said, rolling over onto his back, one hand over his eyes. She could tell it was a struggle for him to end the encounter so quickly. She felt the same way but was grateful for his restraint. She was on the verge of falling in love with him, there was no denying that any longer, but they were still virtual strangers. She wasn't the kind of woman to rush into physical intimacy, no matter how sexy an image she projected to her fans.

"You're pretty good at it, too," she said, grateful that her voice sounded even halfway normal. "But I don't think we should take it any further right now."

"You don't ask for much, do you?" He rolled toward her. She put her hand on his chest, but there was no need to hold him off. "Don't worry, Kelsey. No matter how much I might want to, I'm not going to rush this."

"It's better if we don't. Not until we figure out what this thing is between us."

"God, I hate being practical and noble."

She wrapped her arms around her knees. She was finding she hated it, too. "It's character-building."

"Yeah, right," Matt grumbled as he levered himself up off the floor. "Since I don't have any clothes to change into, or even a razor or toothbrush with me," he said ruefully, "why don't you go do what women do first thing in the morning, and I'll make breakfast if you're brave enough to turn me loose in your kitchen."

It wasn't what she'd expected. She'd been ready to go into detail why making love to him on her living-room floor would be a bad idea, but instead he made her laugh. "Deal," she said. "I do have the fixings for a basic breakfast. Eggs, bread—in the freezer, along with the butter so I'm not tempted as much—and some homemade peach jam my grandmother made last summer, but that's about all. I told you I don't spend much time here."

"Sounds like plenty if there's coffee to go with it."

"And juice. I have juice."

"Everything I need." He surged to his feet in one smooth movement and pulled her up after him.

"There's a half bath off the kitchen. I think there might even be an extra toothbrush and toothpaste in there from when my nephews and my younger cousins stayed here over Christmas."

"You have a big family, I take it."

She rolled her eyes. "Very big. And they all show up for the holidays. My grandmother insists and when Margaret Mary Kelsey insists on something, she usually gets it. She insisted I buy this house from her brother and his wife when they moved to a condo in Sarasota." She spread her hands. "As you can see, I did as I was told."

"Just like that, without even putting up an argument?"

"Just like that."

He laughed and she fell a little further in love with him. His laughter was even more addictive than his kisses. "I have to meet this woman."

She was glad he didn't ask her why Grandma Kelsey had insisted she buy the house—because it would be a great place to raise a big, noisy, happy family. She hadn't let herself think about the babies she might one day have for a long time, but now when she did, the little ones she pictured had dark hair and brown eyes just like Matt. Too early to go there, Kelsey scolded herself and headed for the shower.

Fifteen minutes later, she was back in the kitchen. Matt was as good as his word and breakfast was ready to put on the table. The eggs were scrambled with a little bit of onion and some pepper cheese that he salvaged from the almost empty fridge. There were tall glasses of orange juice and toast with butter and peach jam, and cups of hot, dark coffee.

They talked while they ate. Well, to be truthful, she talked and he listened. He would answer a direct question, like where were his parents living? Retired to Florida.

Why he went into orthopedic medicine? Because his father and grandfather had both suffered sports injuries in their college days that had affected their quality of life in later years. He liked his practice, he volunteered, but when his student loans were finally paid off he wanted to specialize in sports medicine and less in geriatric hip replacements, which paid the bills but weren't particularly challenging.

When they finished eating, Kelsey propped her elbows on the table and cradled her coffee mug in both hands, allowing herself to indulge in another of her most cherished fantasies. Two people sitting here just as they were, savoring the intimacy of a shared life, watching the day come alive, waiting—for the sound of little feet pattering down the hallway as her babies awoke and came searching for their breakfast and their parents' hugs and kisses.

She almost put the fantasy into words but retained enough self-control not to. After all, this whole relationship…if she could even call it that…was so new, so fragile. Matt was almost as much a stranger to her as she was to him. She couldn't let her emotions get ahead of her. That way lay heartache, she was certain of it. They finished their coffee in silence. Matt picked up the dishes and started running water into the sink.

"Leave those. I'll do them later."

"No way. Share and share alike." He squirted soap into the hot water. "What's on your schedule for the rest of the day?" Again a fragment of her domestic fantasy played out before her—sharing chores, sharing plans for the day.

"I have a team meeting at the shop at eleven and then one with my crew chief. I'm supposed to sign autograph requests this afternoon, but I may try to sneak out of that to get in an hour on the simulator."

Matt put down the towel he'd been using to dry dishes and took her hand in his. "Your pulse is racing. You're all revved up already. The race isn't until Sunday. That's a long time to stay excited."

She took a deep breath and made a leap of faith. "It isn't the race I'm excited about. It's my proximity to you." She reached up on tiptoe to give him a kiss.

He took her in his arms and kissed her back. Her toes curled, and her breath caught in her throat. He gazed down as he threaded his fingers through her hair. "Is it really?"

"It's mostly you," Kelsey said, incurably honest. "You know racing is important to me. It's my job and I love doing it."

His eyes were dark and somber, the thoughts hidden behind them impossible for her to read. "There's something special between us. I'm not denying it, but whatever that is, it isn't enough to trump the thrill of going racing, is it?"

She tried for a smile and almost succeeded. "I'd be lying if I didn't say I'm excited about the race this weekend. I'm driving good. I'm feeling good, thanks to you."

He was very quiet now, as stiff and restrained as he had been that first day in the care center at Bristol. What had she said wrong? What had she done?

"And when you feel this way, nothing is going to stand in your way of winning a championship, is there?"

"What are you getting at, Matt?" she asked. Where was this conversation going?

"Is nothing more important to you than winning?"

"There are lots of things, but at the moment my career is number one." She wasn't going to lie to him. Her window of opportunity was very small. She wasn't looking at a twenty-year career behind the wheel. She had other hopes and dreams tucked away inside her heart.

"I was afraid that's what you'd say."

"You don't believe in a woman going after what she wants in life?" Was he an old-fashioned keep-'em-barefoot-and-pregnant throwback? How could she have misread his character so badly?

"Not if she lets her ambitions run roughshod over everything else in her life."

"Including you?" she asked, holding her breath, afraid he wouldn't answer.

"Including me and our baby."

His baby? A shiver of horror coursed down her spine. He turned back to the sink, and she felt the barriers go up between them again. Her heart pounded in her chest, but she tried to remain calm. "Matt, answer me, please. What happened?"

"I don't want to talk about it, Kelsey. I'm sorry I brought it up."

"I do want to talk about it," she said stubbornly. "I can't defend myself if I don't know what it is I've done wrong."

"You haven't done anything wrong."

"Tell me," she insisted. "What was her name?"

"Lisa."

"Did you love her?" That was the most important thing. She had to know that first and foremost.

"I thought I did." So he had loved this woman named Lisa, and she had betrayed him.

"What went wrong between you?"

"She wanted to be a doctor more than anything else in the world."

"What's wrong with that?"

"She wanted it more than she wanted to be my wife." He turned and looked at her, his strong surgeon's hands still buried in the soapy water but balled into fists, the tension in his wrists and forearms plain to see. "More than she wanted to be the mother of our child."

"I don't understand. What do you mean by that?" But she was afraid she did understand and she shivered again.

"Lisa was pregnant. There were problems. The doctors wanted her to go on bed rest. She lost the baby." The words were clipped, diamond-hard, devoid of emotion, but she felt the pain his tone denied.

"I'm sorry, Matt. So sorry." She could barely squeeze the words past the lump in her throat. It was worse, far worse than she'd suspected. Did he really think she was cut from the same cloth as this Lisa? That her life, her hopes and dreams, were centered on a single goal? That she couldn't look past that desire to the future? That she would endanger the life of her child to capture a prize?

Had she been wrong about him? As wrong as he evidently felt he'd been about her? She turned away from the sink, crossed the room to put some distance between them. "It's not all about racing, Matt," she said quietly. "But if you think it is, then I think we've been moving way too fast here."

He dried his hands and folded the dishcloth in two and then once more. He laid it on the counter, aligning the edges just so. He took a step forward and held out his hand as though to reach for her. She backed away another step. If he touched her, she would break into a hundred pieces. She was not like Lisa, but he couldn't see the differences, and she was too proud to point them out.

He pulled his jacket off the hook by the door. "I'll go now."

"Yes, please go."

"Goodbye, Kelsey. Stay safe."

He turned on his heel and opened the door. Tears burned behind her eyes but she refused to let them fall. "Matt," she said, her pride insisting she remain silent, her heart forcing her to speak.

"Yes?" He didn't turn around.

"Just so you know, I'm not Lisa. I'm not like her. I would never do what she did. I would never make that kind of choice."

CHAPTER THIRTEEN

"MATT, SHE'S NOT LISA," Jamie said as he swung his long legs onto Matt's desk and crossed his booted feet at the ankles. He'd come roaring into the parking lot of the clinic on his vintage V-twin shortly after Darla had exited that same parking lot. Matt suspected his friend had timed his arrival deliberately to avoid any meeting with his aunt, who never hesitated to point out to his friend that neuro-surgeons were too valuable and highly trained to be fool-hardy enough to ride motorcycles—helmet or no helmet.

"I know. I didn't want to say what I did to her. I wanted to make love to her. I wanted to tell her I think we belong together, but when she started talking about racing, win-ning a championship," he said, raking his hand through his hair, "all I could think about was Lisa insisting she could do it all, have it all."

"Okay. We've established that point. You choked. You screwed up. But you're not going to give up. We need to come up with a plan to get you back into the lady's good graces, and maybe even into her—"

Matt pivoted on one heel, scowling. Jamie held up a hand in surrender. "Got ya," he said, grinning. "You do have it bad, don't you?"

"I'm pretty sure I'm in love with her," Matt said, for

once having no trouble getting the words past his lips. "I knew that the minute I turned my back on her and walked out the door."

"Then quit feeling sorry for yourself and go after her." Jamie held up an expensive sheet of writing paper that he'd removed from its matching envelope. "An invitation to join Milo and Juliana Grosso for dinner. Tonight, in their motor home, *inside* the VIP lot at Richmond."

Matt frowned. "I barely know them."

"So what? You treated the old man last year, I remember you saying so. You checked Justin Murphy out after that pileup at Bristol. He's family. They want to thank you. What's wrong with that? Take it as a sign from heaven," he said, grinning. "This is your excuse for going, so drive yourself up to Richmond and get your girl back."

Matt did his best to tamp down the flare of hope that seared his gut. "I have two hip-replacement patients still in recovery."

"I'm on call this weekend. I'll take your patients. Next objection?"

"The invitation is from the Grossos, not from Kelsey."

Jamie slapped his forehead in disgust. "I'm not hearing this, right? Okay, Lisa did a number on you. She wasn't the woman you thought she was. Your heart got broken, but it's time to move on, man. You've found a woman who must be something pretty special if you're already more than half in love with her. You owe it to yourself—you owe it to her— to find out for sure." He stood up and pushed the envelope containing Juliana Grosso's invitation toward Matt. "Don't screw this up." He picked up his helmet and sauntered toward the door. "Give my service the details on your patients. I'll check in on them first thing in the morning."

"DR. ABRAMS? MATT?" A golf cart pulled alongside him as Matt exited the credentials hauler at the racetrack. The man driving the cart was about his own age. Even though he was wearing a long-brimmed ball cap and aviator-style sunglasses Matt had no trouble recognizing Kent Grosso, the former NASCAR champion and one of the early season favorites to make the Chase for the NASCAR Sprint Cup again this year.

"I'm Matt Abrams."

"I'm here to pick you up and take you to my great-grandparents' motor home."

The NASCAR Nationwide Series race had ended while Matt was filling out the paperwork for his credentials. People were moving steadily toward the exits, and the overwhelming roar of the engines had faded enough to be replaced by ordinary crowd noise.

"How did you know I was here?" he asked, removing his own sunglasses. It was a sultry spring afternoon. There was a threat of thunderstorms for later that night, but for the moment the May sun was bright in the sky.

Kent jerked a thumb toward the building. "My great-grandmother asked them to let us know when you were inside the track."

"I'm grateful for the invitation and this." He flicked the credential holder affixed to a lanyard around his neck. "But I haven't the slightest idea why your great-grandparents invited me here this weekend."

"You'll have to take that up with Nana. I'm just the chauffeur," Kent said, grinning. "Hop in."

Matt decided to give up asking questions Kent couldn't, or wouldn't, answer. He swung into the passenger seat of the cart and settled back to enjoy the ride. They wound their way through the moving sea of pedestrians and hurrying team members to a fenced-in VIP area filled with high-end motor homes and guarded by a duo of security guards that would have done justice to an NFL team's offensive line.

Kent slowed the cart but the guards waved him through with barely a glance at their credentials. Matt doubted that would have been the case if he'd shown up without one. They passed through the gate the guard held open and thirty seconds later came to a halt in front of a kind of courtyard made by an awning affixed to two of the big diesel units. "The Grosso compound," Kent said with a wave of his hand. "My family's homes away from home."

Shaded from the bright afternoon sun by the canvas, folding tables and chairs held an assortment of people ranging from drivers, whose faces Matt recognized, to crew members in team uniforms, to people like himself dressed in khakis and polo shirts. Everyone was eating, helping themselves from a buffet set up at the back of the space. Small children darted in and out among the tables, and no one seemed to mind them being there. Conversation was animated and only one or two people paid more than passing notice to his arrival.

"My great-grandparents are inside. I'll let them know you're here and then we'll get you something to eat. Nana, Milo," he hollered through the open door, "Here he is." He motioned Matt ahead of him.

"Dr. Abrams, so glad you could make it." Juliana Grosso came out from behind the counter in the kitchen area of the surprisingly large and well-appointed motor home.

"Thank you for inviting me," he said automatically. Her hair was upswept in the style he'd come to associate with her and as with the other times they'd met, she was wearing half a dozen bracelets and rings on every finger.

"Excellent. Thank you, Kent. Close the door behind you, please, so we can have a little privacy. I'll send our guest out to join you presently." Kent touched his finger to the bill of his ball cap in a little salute and backed down the steps, closing the door as he'd been told.

"Milo, wake up. Our guest is here."

"I'm awake. You don't have to shout," a grumbling voice said from one of the two overstuffed recliners in the salon of the motor home.

Juliana motioned Matt to a seat on the sofa. The recliner swiveled to show a small, wizened, nearly bald old man with sharp, intelligent eyes. It had been more than a year since Matt had treated the ninety-year-old patriarch of the Grosso clan but he hadn't seemed to change a bit.

"It's a pleasure to see both of you again. Please, Mr. Grosso, don't get up."

"I don't intend to," Milo retorted, holding out his hand. "One of the perks of being older than dirt is that you don't have to mind your manners any longer."

Juliana rolled her eyes. "Milo, behave."

"Have a seat," Milo said. His grip was surprisingly strong for a man his age. "I imagine you're wondering what you're doing here?" he asked without preamble or small talk.

"I don't know why you invited me but I'm grateful to be here."

"Tell me your gratitude isn't just because you get to see the race?" Juliana asked coyly.

He considered pretending not to understand what she meant but he knew enough about her to know she would have the truth out of him sooner or later. He decided to make it easy on himself. "You're correct. I would have done my damn—my best—to get this far but I doubt I would have succeeded without your help."

"I knew it, Milo. I knew it. He's come after Kelsey, haven't you?"

"Yes," Matt said.

"My wife fancies herself a matchmaker, Dr. Abrams," Milo stated bluntly.

"I prefer to think of myself as a romantic facilitator," Juliana said, smiling. "We're both fond of Kelsey. We want to see her happy. Our Sophia says she hasn't been happy these past couple of weeks. It wasn't hard to figure out why."

"She's a great girl, and a hell of a stock-car driver," Milo grumbled. "We don't want to see her hurt. You aren't trifling with her, are you, son?"

"Hush, Milo," Juliana said, giving him a tap on the arm. But both Milo and his wife were watching him intently. Matt decided not to play with words. "I came to tell her I love her and that I want to spend the rest of my life with her, if she'll have me."

"Excellent! See, Milo, I told you this was the right thing to do." She stood up. "We've given you a little help by providing the credentials, but rest assured that's all the interfering we'll do. You are free to make your own destiny."

Milo snorted again. "Tone it down, Juliana, my love," he said reprovingly but with a smile in his eyes.

Juliana laughed. "I'm sorry. But I mean it. You're on your own from now on. All I can tell you is this. Kelsey's motor home is directly across the row and two to the left. She's at a sponsor shindig right now but she'll be back within the hour. What you do with that information is up to you." She stood up and Matt rose, too, feeling a little shell-shocked. "Come along. Let's get you something to eat. We won't speak of this again, but if it all works out as I hope it will, you'll invite us to the wedding, won't you?"

CHAPTER FOURTEEN

KELSEY PULLED HER GOLF cart into the small space in front of her motor home and picked up her helmet. It had been a hectic day filled with qualifying: she'd been ninth-fastest and would start on the inside of the fifth row for tomorrow's race—not bad, not bad at all; last-minute adjustments to race strategy; media conferences; and a visit to a long-term care facility for children whose physical disabilities made it impossible for their families to care for them at home. It had been a tough couple of hours but she wouldn't have missed it for the world. The kids were upbeat and excited, their caregivers friendly and affectionate. She'd posed for pictures, autographed hats, hero cards and casts. She'd laughed a lot, cried a little, promised to return for the fall race and came away tired but exhilarated.

She heard the music coming from the direction of the Grosso motor homes and considered joining the party but she'd promised herself a long hot shower, a glass of wine and an early night. Her good showings in the past few races had increased her confidence in her driving skills, but tomorrow she was short-track racing again. Despite her good qualifying run, it would take all her energy and concentration to stay in the hunt and out of the wall.

She reached up and touched the back of her neck. She

could feel tension begin to radiate into her nerve endings. She stopped and took a deep breath, let it out slowly, drew in another. Deep-breathing exercises were now part of her daily routine. Her physical pain was gone, but the pain in her heart since Matt had walked out of her life was far worse than the pain in her neck and shoulders had ever been, and far more likely to never be cured.

But she'd promised herself not to think about Matt. Not until the race was over and done. She could force her day-time thoughts about him into a cage at the back of her mind, but her dreams were another matter entirely. In her dreams, he came to her every night. Maybe she would have two glasses of wine, she decided. That might help her to sleep so deeply she didn't dream at all. To achieve that goal, she would definitely need a second glass of wine. She had tucked her helmet under her arm and lifted her hand to punch in the key code on her security system when she heard a man's voice speak her name.

Matt.

It couldn't be. He was back in Concord.

She froze where she was standing then gave her head a little shake. She did have it bad if she imagined him calling her name on the twilight breeze so vividly it sounded real.

"Kelsey." The exasperated note in the male voice was familiar and very real.

She turned her head. He was standing there, not ten feet away, wearing khakis and the leather jacket that looked so good on him. He was real, solid and substantial and entirely male, not a fantasy or a dream.

"Matt? Where did you come from?"

She shifted her gaze to the lanyard around his neck. With credentials and an escort he'd had no trouble getting in to this very private enclave. "Sophia?" It would be like her friend to start matchmaking in the family tradition.

"Juliana and Milo." She looked past him to see the elderly couple standing at the edge of their makeshift patio. Juliana waved and Milo raised his hand in salute; then they turned back to their guests, arm in arm. Matt waited until she shifted her gaze back to him and then took a step forward. "I was coming anyway. They just made it easy for me. I was hoping I could impress you by storming the VIP compound like some NASCAR version of a knight in shining armor."

She laughed. "More likely I would have had to come bail you out of the security holding cell."

"Would you have done that, Kelsey?"

She wasn't laughing anymore. She didn't have the breath for it. Her heart was beating hard and fast in her chest. "Why are you here, Matt?"

"Because I was a fool and a coward when I walked out on you that morning without giving you a chance to tell me more about yourself, your hopes and dreams. Because I couldn't forget the past long enough to ask what you wanted from the future."

"I told you I wouldn't—"

"Let me finish, Kelsey. Please."

She nodded for him to continue. She couldn't trust her voice.

"I don't want you to give up racing," Matt said. "Not now, not until you're ready. But I think you want the same things I do from the future—a lover, a partner, a home and family. Tell me I'm right about that."

"I want all those things," Kelsey whispered.

"You're not Lisa," he said.

His face was hidden by the shadow cast by the big motor home. She wished she could look into his eyes, decipher the emotions hidden there. But she could not so she spoke from her heart.

She shook her head. "No, I'm not Lisa. I tried to tell you that but you weren't listening."

He took another step forward, took her helmet and laid it on the folding chair sitting by the steps. He took her hands between his and held them to his chest. "I'm listening now. I love you, Kelsey. I can say that without equivocation because I thought I was in love once before and I was wrong. What I feel for you is different, is real and true. I'll love you and support you in whatever path you want your life to take, just as long as we can travel that road together." He leaned forward, rested his forehead against hers. "I know this is sudden, Kelsey. I know I haven't given you much chance to fall in love with me but tell me you'll think about it—"

"I don't need to think about it. I love you, too."

She freed her hand and placed her fingers against his lips. "Come inside. We have a lot to talk about. We have our whole lives to plan."

CHAPTER FIFTEEN

"KELSEY, GREAT RACE. Second-fastest. You've had a good run since Martinsville, two top twenties and a top ten at Talladega. But this is your first top-five finish in a Sprint Cup car. How does it feel?"

Kelsey dropped her helmet through the open window of her race car, tugged a PDQ Racing ball cap on her head that one of the PR people slapped into her hand and flipped her hair over her shoulder, giving the TV pit reporter her best smile. She didn't have to fake it. She felt like smiling, like dancing, like flying, even though she'd just finished a grueling five-hundred-lap race.

"It's fantastic, Barry," she shouted over the roar of race engines as cars returned to the garages to be loaded onto their haulers for the trip back to North Carolina. "The car was great. The team was great. I have a great sponsor and a great crew chief and a great team owner. What more could a girl ask for?"

"That's a lot of greats," the reporter grinned back at her. "Is everything else great in your life, too?"

The crowd encircling them eddied and swirled, parting for a moment to allow her a glimpse of the tall, dark-haired man she'd been searching for. Her smile didn't falter, but inside her heart gave a great lurch and began to beat faster.

Matt. Her Matt.

He was standing there, patiently—or perhaps not so patiently, she noticed—as he removed his aviator-style shades and met her glance head-on for a moment. If he kept that up, she was going to need a restrictor plate to slow down her pulse.

She smiled again and spoke from her heart, not to the reporter but to the man she loved. "Finishing in the top five was a great accomplishment for me, one of my goals. My next is to win a Sprint Cup race—a lot of Sprint Cup races, but winning isn't everything."

She excused herself from the reporter and began to make her way through the crowd until she stood toe-to-toe with Matt. He was dressed in the same khakis and a polo shirt he'd worn the day before. He'd been so determined to get to her he'd driven to Richmond without even packing an overnight bag. She liked that.

His hot pass dangled from a lanyard around his neck. He had come to find her on his own but he wouldn't have gotten any farther than the grandstand if it hadn't been for Juliana providing the magic key to her NASCAR world. She would always be grateful to both Juliana and Milo for making her happily-ever-after ending possible.

"I heard what you told the reporter," Matt said, his voice wrapping around her. They stood close but not touching. She wasn't ready for the world to know about them. Her love was too new, too special, to share just yet.

"I meant every word I said."

"I know. We'll make it work. We'll find a way to have it all," he said as the crowd parted around them, giving them a moment of privacy. It was a promise.

"Yes," she said, smiling—her own smile, the one she gave from her heart. "We'll have it all."

* * * * *

HARLEQUIN®

A Romance

FOR EVERY MOOD™

Spotlight on
─ Heart & Home ─

Heartwarming romances
where love can happen
right when you least expect it.

See the next page to enjoy a sneak peek
from Silhouette Special Edition®,
a Heart and Home series.

CATHHSSE10

Introducing McFARLANE'S PERFECT BRIDE
by USA TODAY *bestselling author Christine Rimmer,*
from Silhouette Special Edition®.

Entranced. Captivated. Enchanted.

Connor sat across the table from Tori Jones and couldn't help thinking that those words exactly described what effect the small-town schoolteacher had on him. He might as well stop trying to tell himself he wasn't interested. He was powerfully drawn to her.

Clearly, he should have dated more when he was younger.

There had been a couple of other women since Jennifer had walked out on him. But he had never been entranced. Or captivated. Or enchanted.

Until now.

He wanted her—*her,* Tori Jones, in particular. Not just someone suitably attractive and well-bred, as Jennifer had been. Not just someone sophisticated, sexually exciting and discreet, which pretty much described the two women he'd dated after his marriage crashed and burned.

It came to him that he…he *liked* this woman. And that was new to him. He liked her quick wit, her wisdom and her big heart. He liked the passion in her voice when she talked about things she believed in.

He liked *her.* And suddenly it mattered all out of proportion that she might like him, too.

Was he losing it? He couldn't help but wonder. Was he cracking under the strain—of the soured economy, the McFarlane House setbacks, his divorce, the scary changes in his son? Of the changes he'd decided he needed to make in his life and himself?

SSEEXP0710

Strangely, right then, on his first date with Tori Jones, he didn't care if he just might be going over the edge. He was having a great time—having *fun*, of all things—and he didn't want it to end.

Is Connor finally able to admit his feelings to Tori, and are they reciprocated?
Find out in McFARLANE'S PERFECT BRIDE by USA TODAY *bestselling author Christine Rimmer.*
Available July 2010,
only from Silhouette Special Edition®.

Copyright © 2010 by Christine Reynolds

SSEEXP0710